Pied Piper's
PRINCE

GINA LYNELLE SCHAEFER

Dedicated to the loves of my life, my husband Gary, and my son Gary Joseph.

Special Dedication to any of the lives you have been touched by the true story behind the fiction. My love and prayers are with you.

Prologue

On August 8th, 1973, a young man called the Pasadena Police Department in Pasadena, Texas. He had just shot and killed a man that was attacking him and his two friends. The story would eventually unravel the mystery of numerous missing boys in the Houston and Pasadena areas in the great state of Texas. The story will also coin the term serial killer. During the investigation the secrets of torture and murder were unfolded. Reporters from all around the nation and true crime writer Truman Compote showed up to see if they could capture the 'story of the year' or the next best seller. This, however, is not that story.

The Pied Pipers Prince is a fictional tale, and a twisted one. Admittedly there are grains of the horrific event as well as considerations of others where mothers and fathers have had to say goodbye to a memory instead of a recovered body. Their last shreds of hope washed away by tears as each boy or in some cases, a portion of a boy was uncovered.

Although this book instills a bit of madness, the grief that one feels from losing a loved one in such a horrid way is to not be disrespected. It has been nearly fifty years since that phone call, and with many of the family members having moved on or passed away, it remains a stain on Texas History that has been covered up with live music and Barbecue. Sadly, there are no markers of remembrance or talk in the Pasadena or surrounding areas of what would become known as the Houston Mass Murders, but occasionally there will be a show of the Lost Boys that will pop up, usually every time the house on Lamar Street is listed for sale raising morbid curiosities of wanting to be near a place where so many murders took place, or a parent of one of these children passes away hoping that their long lost son will meet them at Heaven's Gate.

As you weave your way through another twisted tale of paranormal horror and demonic vengeance, take a breath away from the fantasy within these pages and love those around you. Pray for those that have had their children's lives stolen from them by the real evil of the world and if you have had a life touched in such a horrible way, the author's prayers are with you and your family.

1

The Pied Piper's Prince

My name is David. Or at least that is what I recall. My brain is lost in a fog. There are times I can barely see my own feet, much less get a thought straight. The last day that I have a clear memory of was May 17, 1970. Well, snapshots of May 17. I don't remember much after that. Before that, glimpses of an existence I think I had, or perhaps, I just made up. It seems that as time goes on, the visions get dimmer. I kinda lost track as to what was real and what fillers I put in my brain. That is what my mom calls it, fillers. You see, sometimes my dreams would seem so real that I was convinced that they really did happen but when I would go and tell my mom about it and she say something like, No David, that is not right. Your imagination is catching up to ya, cuz you got fillers in your head now.' If she knew about all the pot that I smoked, she would blame that, but fortunately she doesn't know, or I would have to hear her wail in sorrow about where she went wrong and stuff like that. Most the time though, I think that maybe I am just doomed to have a bad memory.

I get flashes though. Not like lightning flashes or anything poetic like that, but more like when you turn on a black and white tv and it thinks about coming on, but it makes a static noise and there is a line in the middle before it decides if it wants to give you a clear screen with visible black, white, and grey pixels or you get the sound bursts and then a buzz with the flickering line. Not sure if the tv will come to life or if it is gonna just fizzle out right there. That is how my mind works. I will try and tell my story, through the flickering line, and the low buzz sound that echoes in the world. Can you hear it? The sounds of echoes in the air. It is all I hear along with the smell of tar and fog capturing my lungs mixed with the smell of old stale blood.

Did you know that? That blood can get stale I mean? That is what gets me the most is the smell of blood. You would think it would be sticky to walk on, but I don't feel it anymore. I figure if I pretend like it isn't there than it will eventually not be there. Just some disgusting pattern blended into the fibers of the carpet. I know this all sounds disgusting and maybe it is, but please don't judge before you know my story. You see, when your story is a culmination of moments of time where you are not sure how they connect, you make yourself get use to a lot of things.

The air didn't always smell like smokey tar hosed down with fog. I remember a beautiful day. Listening to The Box Tops singing Cry for My Baby while working at the bone yard. Yeah, the job wasn't great, but it was close to home and Benny paid pretty good. He'd also cut a deal with anyone for car parts no matter the condition. I saw him once, give Tony, a boy that would come to see his dogs, couldn't have been more than eight, Benny gave that kid a quarter for one of his hot wheels cars that had a broken wheel. Now that is what I call a good guy.

All the local truckers, and towers always dropped of their old engine junk to him. Course he didn't see it as junk. To him, it was all greased-up treasures. A muffler there, a fuel pump here. Some cars torn apart weren't even made anymore but he didn't care. He never turned a piece away and nobody left without at least a dime. I think I miss him the most outside my mama and my brother Ralph. Don't know my daddy and I don't care. Mom took care of us just fine, but the arthritis got into her fingers, and she can't sew or clean houses the way she used to so that's why I work at Benny's bone yard. He treats me good, and his wife is always making pies or boxing up bags of lemons and peaches for me to take home to Mom and Ralph. Good people they are. The grain of the American Earth, my mom says. She says lots of fancy sayings like that. Half the time, I don't quite know what they mean, but I know if I did, I would know that the words were real special just like her. Not like mine. You see my words aren't as clear as my thoughts. I stutter. Stuttering Sam, the kids at school would call me. Although, my name ain't Sam, but I do stutter. Pretty bad too.

Across from the yard is a middle school called Harvis. Not sure why they called it that. Usually, schools around here are named after someone real special or famous or something. Not sure how you go about getting a school named after you. I don't imagine one will be named after me any time soon. Cuz, I'm not special, unless you ask Mom but, I'm certainly not famous, unless you call being known by an entire fifth grade as Stuttering Sam. But I'm not in fifth grade anymore. I just turned twenty. I am a full-grown man, but I still live with Mom and Ralph cuz they need me, and I guess if I thought about it long and hard, I need them too. Course, I don't think I have been home in quite some time.

Anyway, Harvis is where Jeremy goes to school. That's Benny's son. He's a good kid but Benny and his wife Rose are awfully worried. Jeremy didn't come home straight after school like he normally does. I went to look for him. I asked the crossing guard who told me to go check with the Candy Man who told me to check at the 7-Eleven but the clerk had just begun for the day and he didn't know a Jeremy that came in for a Coke so I went back to Benny's and called Mom from there to see if Ralph had seen him cuz they use to be friends but now not so much cuz of a girl. He hadn't seen him and even though he was real mad at him, he promised he would tell me if he had. Ralph is good like that.

Police wouldn't do nothing about it. Said we had to wait for a few days but Rose, well she wasn't having it. She started a search party. Not sure how she managed to put it together so quickly through her tears, but she did, and I helped. Mom came too, hoping to calm Rose down, and even Ralph got on his bike and rode around the neighborhood for almost two hours. He came home to go to the bathroom and was going to go out again, but Mom said no cuz he could be the next missing kid. I always thought that was kind of funny cuz nobody ever went missing around here. They just went out, and sometimes kids would stay out longer than other kids but then they would come home, usually by the time the streetlights came on but if they didn't then their Moms would holler at them and if they were real late they might get beat by the belt if their daddy did that kind of thing and then they go to school the next day as usual. Nobody ever went missing. Well, not until May 17, 1970.

You know how the sky goes grey right before it rains. It can be hot as a hell basket, course that ain't saying much for Texas because let's face it, we don't hardly know nothing but hot. Just some days are hotter than others and the weather give you warning signs. Like when it is gonna rain. The clouds go grey, and the trees whisper together real quiet like before the first crack of lightening followed by the applause of thunder. That is how it was in our neighborhood, Garden Center. Least from what I can remember. Jeremy was gone for three whole days before the police started knocking on doors. Benny only came in once during that time. Hollering out cuss words, cuz they, 'they' meaning the police were labeling Jeremy as a runaway which is real funny cuz to my knowledge, Jeremy ain't got no problems at home with his parents. He just had problems. Not like mine. Mine has to do with the learning. I don't learn too good. But Jeremy, well he's real smart. He just can't breathe to well. Has to have an inhaler. He wouldn't go too far without medicine. Especially now since his breathing gets a lot worse with the allergy season and all. The last time I remember seeing Rose and Benny was when I went to their house. Mama sent some food because she knew there was no cooking going on there. Not with Jeremy gone and all and well, people, even scared ones got to eat. So, Mom cooked, and I brought them the food. Meatloaf and mash potatoes and gravy. Mom made great meatloaf. I know meatloaf is just a wad of cooked meat, but she threw in tomato sauce, and that made it taste nice and moist. Especially with a glob of sweet syrup on it. I love syrup on my meatloaf.

I hung my head low when I saw Rose. Never seen a woman in so much pain. I don't think Mom was in that much pain when daddy left. But Rose, well she had a whole new level of pain. Something that filled the air and cut into your heart. I hung my head down, couldn't look at her in that pain. Afraid it would infect me somehow like the measles or something.

Even as I walked home, kicking the dust on the curb, not looking up the pain clung to me. I didn't even see the Candy Man when he drove up in his old Plymouth and offered me a ride. He even held out a beer to me, treating me like I'm a real man. Now don't get me wrong. I ain't exactly the beer drinking, kind in account of how my mind don't always work right. But it was nice to be recognized as someone that could hold their liquor even though the only times that I drank, was on dares in high school. I just like to smoke pot from time to time but I didn't see any of that in the car. Still, I said no at first.

You see, I was gonna keep on walking, just in case I saw Jeremy coming around the corner or something. His parents are a rightful mess and that's when Cory, that's the Candy Man's name, Cory, Cory told me that he knew where Jeremy was. That he was staying right there with him cuz he wasn't doing well in school and he's afraid his parent's will be pissed at him or something. Now that I think about it, that doesn't sound right. Jeremey was smart. He is always talking it up with all his A's and high B's, but that thought didn't hit me until later.

Well, I got all excited. I told him that his parents were really scared and they ain't gonna care about his grades. They just want him home. That's when Cory suggested that I take a ride with him, to his house so that I can tell Jeremy that myself. He said the kid would be more likely to believe it coming from me since I am such a close family friend and all.

Well, I never thought of it like that. That I could be anyone's family friend. I mean, friends weren't something that I really felt that I had on the account of my stutter and all. But I knew Jeremy liked me and I liked him, and I thought, well, I could be the hero that brought Benny's and Rose's son home and that would bring about a happy ending to this nightmare that everyone was going through. So, I jumped right into that nasty old Plymouth. I didn't even let the smell of stale beer gross me out or nothing.

Now, at the time I didn't know Cory that well. I knew that the kids in the neighborhood liked him which could explain why Jeremy would show up to his house. A lot of kids liked him cuz he would pass out candy from his mom's candy shop. That is how he became known as the candy man. But I didn't know him any other way. Well not until the day I slid into his car. He looked at me all wide-eyed. Told me I looked like a prince out of a fairy tale. I laughed and told him that was my name. David Prince but my grandma always called me her little prince on account of my blue eyes and blond hair cuz she said that was the recipe to make someone charming. I told him how she would tell me that one day I was gonna make the girls swoon after me, but that hadn't happened yet. There was still time though, Mom would say.

All Cory said was that I was gonna be his prince, which I thought that was a weird thing to say, but like I said, I didn't know him to well and he wasn't from Texas originally so he probably didn't know that words like that from one man to another would get his ass beat. I didn't have a daddy to tell me those things, but I hung around Benny long enough to pick up on a thing or two. Anyway, I wouldn't do that to the Candy Man cuz he was going to help me find Jeremy and then I would be a hero. Besides, I'm not what you would call the fighting kind.

We weren't far from his house. Just down the street. I remember thinking how odd it would be that I would find him just the block over from his parents and only two blocks from the boneyard. But there we were. He gets out and I follow, just looking at the house. I can't remember why; but I remember having a pain in the pit of my stomach. Kind of like you get when you are hungry but everything you eat or think about eating makes your stomach hurt. But Cory, he put his hand on my shoulder, firm like. He was strong. At least a foot taller than me and guided me towards the door. His grip was so hard I about stumbled on my own feet.

The inside of his home was dim and smelled bad too. Didn't care though, remember, I'm gonna be a hero. I called out, "Jeremy."

"Right back there," Corey said pointing to the back room.

"Jeremy!" I called out again. I rushed to the back of the house but all I saw was a mess. Beer bottles and chip bags littered his living room. It kind of looked like a he just had a party or something. I threw open the door of the back bedroom and slipped. There was this heavy plastic on the floor, guess he was getting work done or something, but it was hard to walk on. I pushed myself up a bit and my eyes focused on two sheets of plywood that was leaning up against the wall. The smell was worse in there. As I was pushing myself up, I felt a heavy weight right between my shoulder blades.

Now this is where my brain starts to become like popcorn. You see, I remember the day I went there, but I don't remember exactly how it went down that I would stay with him. I must have drunk some of those beers that Cory offered me cuz I know that my head hurt and then fogged up. At one point, I thought I saw Jeremy. Walking around all confused. He was hurt. I know that cuz I saw what looked like blood dripping from his ear. I called out to him. I wanted to tell him that his mom wants him at home. She doesn't care about his grades, but I don't know if he ignored me or if I wasn't able get the words out. You see, my brain don't work right. I do remember Cory whispering to me again that I was his prince. His beautiful prince and he was gonna keep me for a while kneeling down pressing himself on me. I must have been hurt cuz I just lied there and when he spoke or stroked my hair, I don't remember the touch. Maybe I blocked it out cuz where I came from, boys don't do that to other boys. I guess it is a good thing that I don't remember his touch cuz I liked it when Mom stroked my hair when I was little and sang and read to me and when nana called me her little prince, but I don't like Cory calling me that because only my nana can call me her little prince.

I only know that darkness came and passed because the streaks of light through the windows. I know Mom was worried about me cuz before Cory said he was gonna keep me close cuz I was his prince; he gave me a postcard to write out. It was an Austin postcard. One with the capital on it. He told me to write her a note that I was going there for work, but I know that if I was doing that, she wouldn't like that. Preston Smith was the governor, and she didn't like Preston Smith. Said he was bad people creating bad politics so I know she would be mad if I was in Austin. The same city as Preston Smith. But I remembered I wrote the note so he would take the tape off my mouth but I didn't know how to spell some of the words so I just did the best I could. That is when I decided that I was scared of Cory, and I still wasn't sure where Jeremy was.

I remember most of that part. Nobody else there except for maybe Jeremy, but I am not sure if he really was there. I just saw a few shadows peering down on me through the fog, but I couldn't make out any faces. Just Cory's and his began to scare me more and more.

He had taken some of those bracelets, you know, like the police use and he attached me to one of those pieces of plywood for a time. Swear I remember that. The board had those knot holes in it that looked like eyeballs that you could see through to the other side. That is how he pinned me down at first until he moved me to the smaller bedroom. There he left me on a mattress. No sheets or nothing Just a smelly mattress that had dark stains and loose threading. He didn't seem to mind though because that is where he would lay down with me.

One day when he was holding me close, he told me he had to leave me behind cuz he got a new job, and he would have to move. I was happy cuz I thought that meant I would be able to go back home to Mom but even though he stopped laying down with me, I stayed with him. In the new place, I paced the floor back and forth, but he didn't pay me any mind. He went about his business. I think he missed the candy company because he had a lot of friends that he would give candy too and now he didn't have any candy to give. After a while, he brought new friends over to the new place. It wasn't much different. He still kept the boards with the shiny bracelets...handcuffs, that's what you call them, handcuffs.

Thank you for your patience. As I said, I don't learn to good, and I definitely don't remember to good. Accept Mom and Ralph. I always remember them and wonder how much time has gone by and if they ever went to Austin to find me.

I know that Cory had another friend named David. I can remember that cuz my name is David too, but I don't recall him referring to him as his prince. I guess you can only have one prince. Besides, most of the time he referred to him as Boozer. Not sure why, but it seemed that was what everyone called him. There were times that I wanted to whisper in Boozer's ear to get out of there and I tried too. I guess he had real bad hearing because he never paid any mind to me.

Boozer was just the beginning of a long line of friends that Cory had. Some of those friends would talk to me but not for long. Sometimes they would talk to me in pairs. This one time, these two guys asked me how to get out. I tried to show them the door, but they had another way out. They didn't bother to come back for me. I sure wish they would have.

Cory wanted his home to be a welcoming place, I guess. You know a place where runaways can go. Why wouldn't they? I mean he was always offering things up like beer and pot to all the boys around. I didn't recognize most of them, but they sounded like they were all around here. Accents like Ralph and Mom. Not like his. Anyway, these boys will get so wasted to the point that they would pass out. It was like Cory had his own little hippie commune right there. He'd get Boozer and Willie, another one of his special friends to invite their friends over and they would have a party almost every night. I guess that Boozer and Willie were special too but not a prince like me. Cory didn't keep the rest of the friends around for as long. Not like them. They did favors for him and well, I'm a prince but I don't have any real interaction with them, and I am totally fine with that.

You know sometimes his special friends would come in all frazzled with their eyes open wide and their hair all sticking out telling Cory that they got to stop. That there were posters all over the place looking for the boys that they brought to him, but Cory would offer them more money to keep on bringing them. Can you believe that. I remember that part now. It's kind of fuzzy but I remember that one time, Cory told Boozer that if he kept his mouth shut and do as he asked, he would give him two hundred dollars for every special friend that he would bring over. I think Boozer was always a little uneasy about the agreement, but Willie never seemed to mind. He would say something like "hell, I'll take that money."

Cory must have burned through a lot of hundred-dollar bills cuz the boys kept coming. My memory of them and the goings on is fuzzy though. It's like some of my other memories: snapshots. I saw Cory, strap boys to a board like the one he strapped me too. Maybe the same one. I don't know. It's like my consciousness only comes out at certain times. I didn't watch the games played with the boys. I couldn't remember the games he played with me, but I know I didn't like it. And from the shrieking and hollering that leaked out from the back room, I don't think they like the games either.

One time I felt so bad about all the hollering that I snuck into the room. There were two boys there. Bare-ass naked, duct tape over their mouths, those shiny bracelets holding them onto that board. One pale white, not like white like a sheet but an ashen white, like how cigarettes buds get when they are old. The other, I couldn't see his face to well. He was crying, muffled like, but I could tell by the shake of his shoulders and the red marks of his back, he was pretty scared. I tried to talk to him. "Danny," I say, I knew his name was Danny cuz I heard Cory tell Boozer that when he told him to bring him back. Anyway, I got close to him and spoke right up in his ear, but he acted like I wasn't even there. Scared is all. Just too scared to take notice of the only kindness around him. I thought that maybe I could figure out a way to loosen those, oh what are they called again? Oh yes, those handcuffs. You know, the bracelets. If I could get them off than maybe, he wouldn't be so scared. It can't feel right to be all trapped like that, unable to move. I mean, I guess. I know that I was like that, but I don't remember much. But I can move about the house now. I couldn't get through to Danny though. I also couldn't handle his shrieking, so I left the room the only way I knew how. I would kind of float within myself, so I wouldn't have to see the games going on.

I wonder if Boozer was ever jealous of all the attention that Cory gave to the other boys cuz one time, Cory gave him a car. Looked like a lima bean but it made him happy. Kept him quiet for a while too. It was a strange friendship, that's for sure. Cory treated the boy like a son, accept no daddy I know would ask the kid for special favors the way that Cory did.

2

2001

"Murder house, Murder house,"

Molly flipped off the kids that were mocking her as she got out her groceries. Damn kids. What? They don't have nothing better to do. Then again, shouldn't the landlord let her know what she was renting? Taking a breath, just six months. I only signed a six-month lease. I can do this.

Quickly, Molly manages to get her groceries in through the backdoor and piling her bags on the counter. She then goes to the living room and shuts her curtains before looking around at the sparce living room. Boxes of cheap knickknacks waiting to topple over. No use in unpacking those. Just the bare minimum and I am out of here. Molly takes a deep breath and heads for the kitchen putting away cold items and grabbing a snack cake. Her phone rings. Damn, It's Leah!"

"Hey, girl, you got those pages yet?" Molly grinds her teeth and looks over to her laptop. Still open, the screen dark but waking it up would be no use. The document would be empty.

"Hey Leah, look, I am still trying to get settled in. To top it off the Wi-Fi sucks here. You wouldn't believe what I got myself into."

"Yeah, yeah, yeah. Enough with the excuses. It's been two weeks. Get settled in and send me something. Otherwise, we will have to cancel the contract." Molly takes a breath.

"I'll write through the night."

"Great, you can…" Molly drowns out Leah's words as she is distracted by a thin mist resting in the living room illuminated by natural sunlight and dust particles.

"Okay," Molly says, slowly walking in the mist's direction. "I'll get you something as soon as I can." She hangs up before Leah could respond. She hits the light switch and hears the pop of the living room bulb signaling its death. The mist weaves around the sunlight streaming in through the cracked curtains streaking the tops of unpacked U-Haul boxes. She walks over to the window and peeks outside. The little monsters are gone, and only a few cars are seen coming down the quiet street. Too early for shadows but maybe this place is getting to me.

The kitchen was equally bright with sun coming through a partial glass door, providing an illusion that the kitchen is larger than it is.

A silhouette floats across the landscape of the back yard. Molly rushes out, throwing the door open, stumbling over a dead housewarming plant to shout out, "Hey," but no answer or even any sign of the backyard figure. "Come on back and I'll call the police on you!" she shouts, "you little creepers. I'll give you something to be afraid of when I'm done with you." The echo of silence salutes her with shivers up her spine. Taking a few steps further out, she checks the outside storage shed only to find it locked as always. With no evidence of intrusion, Molly realizes that playing vigilante with the neighbor kids will have to wait for another day.

Retreating back inside she examines her grocery loot. A few inspired vegetables and berries along with red meat begging for a spot between the sodas and an assortment of her favorite Little Debbie's.

"Yes, I'm going to get healthy. I am going to get thin," Molly says out loud frowning at the foreign greens and fruits that became more unappealing with each look compared to the Pizza Hut coupon so proudly stuck on to the fridge with a Bayshore Hospital magnet. "Well, maybe I will get healthy tomorrow." She lifts her phone and punches in the numbers for Pizza Hut. A number she knew better than her own mother's.

"Yes sir, 2020 Winkle Street. No… this isn't a joke. I live here." Molly speedily tapped her fingers on the counter, her frustration intensifying. "For God's sake, I know it is the murder house. Like, thirty years ago, are you gonna bring me my pizza or do I need to send the goblins after ya. I'm sure corporate will want to hear about it if you don't." The mumble that responded back seemed like a yes ma'am, but she wasn't quite sure. If she got her food she didn't care. Pouring a coke, she settles down in front of her computer to wake it up. Barely three pages on her pathetic romance which she already predicts before writing it would end up in the dime location of a Goodwill only to be touched by lonely housewives. But it was work, even though her dominatrix protagonist was not believable, and the helpless lover was a barbie doll cut out of what every woman wasn't.

Pulling out a stress ball from the top left drawer, she studies the page. His long blonde tasseled hair blew into the sea wind while Danielle's green eyes, met his. Nope, nope, nope, too cliché, Molly said out loud, hitting the backward button hard, creating small punching sounds. "Little to Fabio, let's make you exotic, Hispanic, or Cuban or maybe…"

Thump! Molly hears a loud crush coming from her bedroom. What the hell, she gets up cautiously, and softly walks to her bedroom, peeking in before entering. The room untouched. She scans the room, walks to the bathroom, again in perfect shape and walks back into the bedroom again. She sits and opens the nightstand. Her nightly assortment of snacks, Cheetos, chocolate, all the crap she vowed to stay away from, yet it would be a waste to throw it all away. Hello thighs, here I come, she thinks as she crunches down on a Cheeto. She looks up at a long mirror on her bedroom wall, disgusted by her appearance but not convinced enough to leave the chocolates alone. She stuffs two in her mouth, wipes the chip dust from her fingers to her pants and gets up when she hears the doorbell ring.

"Well, welcome." Molly greets him with a fake pleasantness. The pizza boy stood hesitantly on Molly's doorstep. "Come on in, I'll get you some money."

The boy stood still, "I'll wait right here if you don't mind."

"What, you think the house is going to reach out and bite you?" The young delivery driver lets out a hesitant chuckle.

"If you don't mind me asking, why do you live here?"

"I do mind you asking, and you are about to talk your way out of a tip."

The acne stain teen stepped back a little further from the door annoying Molly more, but he stayed silent. Flustered, she gave him the money for the pizza. "Here, take a two-dollar tip, maybe you can start up a grow some balls fund." She then slammed the door hard before he could say anything further.

Molly's tastebuds watered as she walked into the kitchen, hot cheese teasing her nostrils. Grabbing a paper plate from the counter and a wad of napkins, she takes three big slices, extra cheese with ham and pineapple and places it on her plate while looping hot cheese around her finger, licking it before plopping in front of her computer slobbering away, changing her handsome blonde into a olive skinned Spaniard with a brilliant smile but leaving her protagonist female as the exotic beauty of the Ukraine, steadily adding exotica to her words and calories to her thighs. The time ticked away and before she knew it, she had demolished the large pizza and a litter of coke by herself and managed to write thirteen brilliant pages full of her own fantasies romping around a deserted beach with a man she had total control of. She had left off in the story, where the protagonist was explaining that it was not her desire to be supported by a wayward Spaniard but to be a beautiful badass that was completely self-sufficient.

Molly, leans back, lifts her arms over her head and cracks her knuckles, no misogyny here. Getting up, she carefully picks up her paper plate, gets the empty pizza box and glass and cleans everything up by her computer and then her kitchen. Taking the trash outside, she sucks in a hot gentle wind and squints to see that most of the lights in the neighborhood are off, but the streetlights remain on. A symbol of suburban bliss. She looks around to where she thought she saw the shadow earlier, but nothing. "Guess the police won't be called tonight," she says out loud before stepping back inside.

By eleven, Molly was showered and sleepy.
"Sleep come soon please," Molly whispers into the air as she slips into her warm bed with heavy bedding and many pillows. And it did, restful too, until she began to dream.

3

Within the Vale

"NO!" His hand cut against the handcuffs. It's okay Jeff, it will be over soon. David crouched near the boy's head while the monstrous man hovered over, forcing himself upon him with his body while beating him with his left fist. Jeffrey Zarcs, a fifteen-year-old football player and alter server at Saint Pius church cried and squirmed under the weight. David let out a desperate and helpless cry and zoomed out of the room. Please God, Please God, why are you letting this happen? Thinking and praying in urgent pleas.

No answer though. At least none that could be heard over the shrieks coming from the next room. Why can't the neighbors hear? The neighbors! David rushes to the door and works to turn the handle: it doesn't move. He then rushes to the back door, no use, he tugs, the shrieks grow into thunderous roars throughout the house. He runs to the front living room again and bangs on the window, but no sound is made, not even a slight rattle of the glass. He sees a young woman, walking her dog, talking to a mailman leaning out of his car obviously examining her long slender legs.

"In here, come in here," he shouts. The TV flickers but his voice is released as a whisper covered by the music of the Here's Lucy Show. A lighter is wedged in a package of Marlboro Lights. Set a fire, I could set a fire. That will bring help or get Cory off that boy. Maybe, a fire. He reaches for the cigarettes, but he can't grasp them. He squinches his face as the shrieking dissipates into low whimpers. Then silence.

David pulls himself up and for the first time notices a figure. Between the living room and the hallway, stands a woman. Short and plump, wearing a long tee-shirt and socks, only she's not really there. She is transparent. She stares at him, partially frightened but more curious. Her mouth moves, but David can't make out her words. She steps closer, and lets out another panic whisper, "who are you?"

David bleats out, "do something!"

4

2001

Molly's eyes pop open. She sits up, streaks of sweat dance on her brow. She looks around. The room is quiet except the sound of outdoor activity, creeping in. "Shit! Trash." Molly leaps out of bed and dashes through the small house and stumbles out the back door, morning dew soaking through her socks, her dream drifting further from her thoughts with each tug of the trashcan. She barely makes it to the curb when she sees the garbage truck coming through. Damn, they start early around here. She pulls her shirt down as she notices the man standing on the truck watching her. Uncomfortable she backs up the driveway until she feels close enough to run back in the house but not before catching a glimpse of the one man talking to another as they got down to toss bags of garbage into the back of the truck.

Her shower felt cool on her and she tried to relax while pulling together the bits and pieces of her dream that was becoming more difficult to remember. It seemed too real. Her grandmother had always told her that dreams carried messages and regardless of how disturbing they may seem, they shouldn't be ignored because the insight was important.

That does it, book writing will have to wait until this evening. She thinks, I need more freelance work because clearly writing about fantasy sex is not going to pay this month's bills. She pulls herself out of the shower and rumbles through the frustration of a fat girl getting dress.

Everything smart looking was too tight. Overindulgences in pizza and snack cakes. "Guess, I need to hit the gym," she says out loud, knowing that would never happen. She finally decides on some black pants with a black blazer, both feeling snugger than she liked and a white tank top that she would never wear alone as it outlines every bulge from her waist up. The Citizen offices was only ten minutes away but even at nine in the morning, the traffic was heavier than usual. The construction was more intrusive than usual, and the steam stank from the factories heavier than usual.

She always felt more somber when she drove to the paper. Eddie was not like Leah, who encouraged her inner self to come out in her writing. Eddie was a typical conservative newspaper man, the son of a newspaper man and hoped to raise a newspaper child. As time trudges on, his dream becomes dimmer as more and more people were getting their news from the Internet. Molly wondered if by the time, Eddie's son Jake grew up, if newspapers would even exist anymore. Eddie probably wondered that too. Still, her mother loved the fact that she could pick up a Citizen and say hey, you see that byline, Molly Matthews, that's my daughter. She never wanted to do that with the books she released. Smut she would say. Pure smut.

The building was old and gross. Cement steps stained with a black tar like substance that had probably been there for ages. Compliments from the pollution in the air. The inside was not much better. The carpet a green and black Astro-turf form that made the eighties look modern. The entire office smelled like an ashtray and the orange chairs and brown tables looked like it was donated from a seventy's estate sale. The entire city of Pasadena smelled like chemical laced tar with a dash of mold which of course settled inside the older buildings. This whole town is going to die of an asbestos infection.

The office was calm. When she was a little girl, it was her dream to be some type of high influence journalist that would work in a busy office where the sound of pounding typing dominated the air, but this place wasn't even close. Most of the Citizen's reporters were freelancers like her and the people that did work there were either teen interns or overweight fat men cursing and drinking coffee. The first time she entered the building, she was sure that she would see men smoking cigars and wearing fedoras, but her romantic image vanished with the water-stained ceiling tiles and the petri dish carpet.

Eddie spies her coming in and beckons for her to come over. Good sign, when he doesn't have anything for me or he knows it is something I will whine about, he doesn't make eye contact.

"Hey Molly Day, got a story for ya."

"Great and it's Molly Matthews. What's the pitch?"

"The Phillips explosion that happened last year. They are finally settling with the families. I want you to find some of the relatives and have them agree for you to sit down with them for an interview. Keep the story positive. Run with a vibe on how this will bring peace to the family and yada, yada, yada. You know, stuff like that. Don't care how you do it. Just make it sound good."

Molly nodded in agreement keeping an eyeroll hidden. Boring, but at least it is not some dumbass fundraiser for the local shelter. "I'll get right on that." She squints her eyes and Eddie pretends to look busy, probably to get rid of her, but she had other ideas on her mind. "Eddie, you know the house I'm renting?"

"Can't say that I do."

"Yes, you do, 2020 Winkle Street."

Eddie stands up straight and made eye contact with her. "It's understandable if the place has you spooked." Then sighing, "but brick and mortar. That's all it is now."

"Well, I'm not sure if it is the house itself, but the neighbors treat me like a pariah. They point and whisper. Even the kids are afraid to come into the yard." Taking a breath, "Look, I was born in Kansas. My family didn't move here until the eighties and that was over in Spring. I don't know the history, but from the looks that I get, I figure knowing a little something about the place may be a good idea."

"Nah, that's just your journalist curiosity going. Don't pay any mind to it."

"I want to know."

Taking a deep breath, "that house was once occupied by a Cory Dennison." Shaking his head, "I know that you think this is a story, and I suppose it is, but I let's not bring up that nightmare again."

"What is the story?"

Eddie reaches over for an empty coffee cup, takes a swig of air, stares down at the cup and walks to the coffee pot. "In the early 70's Dennison and two teenage thugs killed twenty-eight kids. Maybe more. Many of those murders happened in that house. Don't matter how much time goes by, that place will always be known as the murder house." Eddie studies Molly's face. "Let the story go. No need in bringing up so much sadness again. Hell, the victims have family that live right there in your neighborhood. Let's not bring back those memories. It's best to let things be forgotten."

5

The Pied Piper's Prince

I don't know how much time has gone by since I have been here. But I do know that I've never been away from home for this many sunrises and sunset. Mom and Ralph must be awfully worried about me. And what about Benny? If I don't go back to work soon, he will have to find somebody else to run the boneyard. That wouldn't be any good. I help Mom with groceries and things. Ralph ain't old enough to work and even if he were, I don't think Mom would like that on the account that he is smart and needs to stay in school. Mom says that Ralph has a bright future. I think he probably does cuz he won the sixth-grade spelling bee. He's smart. He doesn't stutter like I do.

I miss them. Like I said, I don't know how much time has passed. I wonder how long somebody needs to be gone for them to be missed. I wonder how long somebody needs to be gone before somebody is forgotten. All I know, is I don't see Jeremy here anymore and I don't think Jeff is here anymore either. He stopped his squealing. I don't no mean disrespect to him cuz I know he was afraid. But he did some squealing. He sounded like a scared pig about to go to slaughter. I don't think that I was ever that scared. Cory didn't want to scare me much cuz I'm his prince.

That's what he said, but I know in my heart that I will never allow myself to be his prince. That's why I ain't jealous when he brings in other people that he is fond of. Course, Cory don't bring in the people himself. He gets his two special friends to bring them in. You see, Cory works during the day but at night he comes home and plays with whatever treasures that Boozer and Willie bought him. It is like one big party every night and sometimes the boys that Boozer and Willie find think they are the guests of honor. Well, until they know what is in store for them.

It goes something like this. Cory brings home the beer and the marijuana and gives all the boys anything they wanted up until they'd get so drunk and high and stupid that they be stumbling all over the place. Then Wille, the sneaky mean one; the one that did most of Cory's bidding, would ask to play a little game with the handcuffs. First time I noticed it was when they brought Frank over.

You see, Frank wanted to be a cop or something. He goes to school with Willie and Boozer, so they know all about it. Apparently, Frank would brag that he could trap anyone, especially the bad guys. I overheard him tell Boozer that it was a great line to get the girls. Anyway, for some reason that peeved Willie off. He showed Frank these handcuffs and put them on and slipped them right off like it was some kind of magic trick or something. Now I could see that Willie had a secret key, but Frank didn't know. Poor kid didn't have a chance. He put those things right on and no sooner that they were on, Cory threw him to the ground and taped up his mouth while Willie tied up his legs. Laughing hysterically like they were in a Cheech and Chong movie or something. That stayed stuck cuz they watched a lot of Cheech and Chong. I know that I said my head gets stuck in the fog, but I remember the Cheech and Chong movies. Willie and Cory really liked them. Boozer wasn't too fond of them, but he would laugh anyhow because he wanted Cory to like him. To think he was special. Now that I think of it, he probably was jealous of me, but Cory talked to him more. Also, gave him gifts along with the money he paid him.

Cory needed Boozer and Willie, but I don't think he ever bothered to tell them. It seems that when he closed the candy shop, he didn't have much of anything to give away. Funny I remember that cuz I don't quite know when he closed the shop and started working for the phone company. Time must be passing quite a bit. I hope Mom didn't forget about me. I would be sad if she forgot about me. Ralph can have my model cars. I don't think I want to play with them anymore when I get back home.

6

2001

August 11, 1973: 2 Houston teens Charged in 3 of 23 Youth Slayings.

Molly looked at the Houston Chronicle headlines, her stomach twisting as she read. Teen boys, children, arrested for kidnapping, conducting sex orgies, and murdering their own friends. Leading the police to unmarked graves of numerous young men believed to have been runaways but were victims of the trio led by Cory Dennison, now dead. Shot down by William Higginbotham. Within a few hours, bodies were recovered in three different locations. One being a public storage shed down the street from where Molly lived. Many of the murders committed at 2020 Winkle Street. The Murder House

Molly sat back, her stomach surged, I do live in a murder house. Molly read further. Dennison had been killing kids even before he moved to the Winkle Street House. Nobody knows how many, with the death of Dennison, the only ones that will be recovered are the ones that William Higginbotham and David aka Boozer Rivers will lead them to. The two surviving boys. The two surviving sadists murderers. Rivers went on to report that he had witnessed killings long before Higginbotham came into the picture. Sometimes he would kill the boys right away and sometimes he would keep them awhile. Torturing them with objects that he made. He even would occasionally hang onto a corpse if he felt a special affection to it. Rivers who would live with him for stints at a time, stated the smell didn't seem to bother Dennison.

"Molly, here is the address of the…" Eddie stopped, "I told you to let it go. It's going to keep you up at night. I need you on this besides."

Molly reached behind her and took the slip of paper from Eddie, her eyes remaining focused on the screen. "Okay, I got this." But she didn't have this. Her mind was captured by the horrific crimes that unraveled in her home.

 "Sorry dude, I'm not letting this go," she said underneath her breath. She got up slowly, took a breath and walked to the coke machine where she numbly dropped two quarters into the slots. Thud, then a jolt sounded. "Damn machine," she pounded on it and then gave it a swift kick.

"Hey, you'll destroy the thing," Billy said with a friendly smile. He was a Citizen photographer that she been on a few dates with. Molly smiled, not really wanting to engage with him.

"Rough morning. Didn't get much sleep last night."

"Sorry to hear that." Billy shook the machine hard enough until a release was heard followed by a clunk. He leans down, pulls out the coke and hands it to her. "I was hoping to run into you. Thought you might want to go to Peppers tonight."

Molly shrugged her shoulders, "I don't know," she paused, "Billy, did you live around here in the seventies. "Been here all my life. Well in the area that is. We moved to Deer Park when I was little, but I know all the town stories."

"Do you remember any talk about the Dennison murders. I mean I know you would have been young, so I understand…" Molly stopped. She noticed Billy shuffling his stance, looking down, in a noticeable uncomfortable position. "Billy, are you all right."

"My brother was one of those boys. I remember all too well. That monster took Charlie away and…" Billy looked to the side not wanting Molly to see the emotion in his eyes.

"Billy, I'm so sorry, I had no idea. I never heard you talk about a brother."

Billy wipes his face with his hand, "well, it was a long time ago." Taking a breath and with a fresh smile, "so how about Peppers tonight?"

7

The Pied Piper's Prince

I've seen a lot of boys come through. We moved a few times, I lost sight of myself, but I am still here. I know now that I have been trapped into staying with Cory although he doesn't pay me much mind. There were a lot of other boys he liked a lot. He liked blonde hair and blue eyes. Sometimes I wonder if this made Cory's friends jealous. Especially Willie. His hair is closer to a brown.

Willie would get kind of crazy sometimes. I think he likes torturing the boys just as much as Cory does. Especially when we were in the small house that we moved into. Not sure if Cory rented it or just took over after his dad left, but that is where Willie went crazy. Cory too for that matter. It was like this glaze would come over their eyes. They would argue who gets to do what with the boys, every time a new one was brought in. The fighting turned into snarling and growling and as it was happening, the whole atmosphere changed. A thickness would come over the room.

I'd admit, I saw everything through a fog, but on some days the fog wasn't as thick. The arguing and the days where a new boy was brought here were the days that the fog was the thickest. Strange how it all worked out. Sometimes they don't have any playmates, and, on these days, they smoke and drink and party but on other days, Cory will get what he calls a hankering, that is what he would say, I have a hankering, and he'd throw some cash at Wille and tell him to take the van out and bring back some fresh meat. And that is exactly what Willie did. Like he was running to the corner store or something. Sometimes, Cory didn't like what he brought back, and he would get mean, but he would still take the meat, as he would say.

Other times, Cory would go with the other two to bring someone back. Said he was more skilled in luring cuz he knows what they like, and that Willie and Boozer are stupid. Except, I don't think they are stupid. I think Boozer just didn't know what to do and well Willie… well I can't really explain Willie. He has a heavy dark shadow following him and it serves as a barrier to his reasoning. I didn't see it at first but now I do all the time. I hate looking at it. I want to hide from it cuz if it knows that I am there, well, it's likely to swallow me up or something. I don't want that. I don't want that at all.

8

2001

"I'm real glad you decided to come out tonight, Molly."

Billy always looked better in dim restaurants. Picture of a nice man. Not too tall but not too short. Heavy set but not as heavy as her and a kind disposition. He had been working for the Citizen since the mid-eighties. Started off as a part-time job while he attended college, but it eventually graduated into a nice career for him. It was curious to her as to why he never married but she couldn't bring herself to ask because that would just lead into a conversation about her two divorces and why she lost custody of her only child. Just the same, he was a good guy and good guys were not easy to come by. She wanted to question Billy about his brother but thought it better not too after the morning's surge of emotions. And when Molly wasn't asking questions, it didn't leave her with much to say. Fortunately, while she was attempting to think of something to say, the dinner arrives.

"That looks delicious," Molly says as she unwraps her silverware, eyeing Billy's steak, and grilled shrimp.

"It is, do you want a bite?"

Molly nods, "no, I've had their spinach enchiladas here before and I know it will more than fill me up." Then cautiously, "so Billy, you grew up around here."

"Yeah, back when it was mostly plants and nothing else. Most of them weren't here even then. Hell, I was sitting in the old Sears parking lot back when Urban Cowboy was filmed. You ever see that show. Gilley's was here too you know."

"I thought you moved when you were young."

"To Deer Park, I still hung around the same kids though. We were all tight back then. I still have buddies that I hung out with since elementary. I can introduce you. Get you some friends here."

"Why Deer Park?" Billy made a face, "you said your family moved to Deer Park. It is such a short distance away."

"Well, I told you about my brother Charlie. When my parents found out what happened to him, and the house where it happened," Molly hung her head down, "well, it was just up the street from where we lived, and mom couldn't take driving past it every day."

"My house, you mean. He was killed in my house."

"Whoa, wait," Billy places his hand on her arm. "That's not your fault. That house you live in, is a building, it has nothing to do with you."

"Doesn't it though. I mean, do you believe that a house can have memories."

Billy chewed his steak slowly, took a sip of his tea, and scratched his beard. He spoke carefully and thoughtfully, "no, I don't believe that. A house doesn't commit a crime, a person does. The day that Cory Dennison was shot down was the last day that house was a part of the gruesome story."

"Then why do you think nobody has lasted in the house for any length of time."

"Because of the same stuff that is spooking you. The history, the murders, the nosy neighbors that feel the need to point and whisper every time you go in and out. My god, that is the part that I don't know how you deal with."

"Tell me about it. Last night the pizza boy wouldn't even come in. Wasn't even sure if he would take my money. Think he thought I was possessed or something." Wiping her lips, she looks up at him, "I do have a question for you though." Billy nods, "last time we went out, you didn't want to come in. You made an excuse."

Billy shakes his head, puts down his fork and looks at a light before looking at her. "I know my brother has passed on. I know that. I also believe that his spirt went straight to heaven, but the idea that his last breath was in that house, after suffering the torture that he suffered, I just couldn't bring myself to go in. You had just moved in, and I didn't want to take your joy. Spoil the mood. Also, wanted you to think of me as a gentleman."

Molly spoke slowly, hoping to get her questions answered while remaining respectful. "I know that there were some horrendous crimes in the house. Boys were strangled and shot. I don't know much about the torture except the ra…" Molly started to say rapes but then stopped herself to reword it to "assaults."

Billy took another sip of his drink, swallowing hard. "Are you planning on doing a story on this or something."

"No, not exactly, I am looking for answers I guess." Then almost whispering, "you may think I'm crazy, but I believe there is something in my house."

Billy squints his eyes, causing Molly to pause, oh, shit, he's gonna think I'm crazy, but before she could break the silence he responds, "Oh, like a ghost. Come on, you don't believe in that kind of stuff do you."

Molly shrugged her shoulders. "I feel like I am going crazy. I think I see things that aren't there, or I hear things and last night I had a weird dream that I barely remember now, although when I woke, it seemed too real for comfort."

"That house is probably getting to you, although," Billy takes a breath, "your neighborhood isn't the best. Have you thought about getting an alarm? Or a dog maybe. You know you may not be seeing things. There could be people poking around your house. Curious crime seekers. It is a notorious house."

"Well from what I read; he didn't even commit that many of the murders there. Just a few and he died there himself."

"Doesn't matter. People get curious over the strangest things. You said yourself that people stop and look at you. Maybe superstitious people wondering how you can bring yourself to live in that house."

"Well, the realtor didn't find it necessary to tell me the house's history and I didn't think to ask, 'hey, was there a serial killer that lived her that raped and tortured his prey before falling to his own demise." As soon as Molly made the comment, she wanted to take her words back. "Billy," she stuttered. "I'm so sorry, that was very insensitive of me and…"

Billy smiled and held up his hand, "no worries, I don't know exactly what happened in that house, but I do know that my brother was subjected to it. I would like to think that he fought back, that his last breath was not in vain but, well… well, I guess that will never be known." Looking up and motioning for the waiter, "would you like to get out of here and take a stroll in Crenshaw Park?" Molly nodded and muttered that would be nice, but her mind was lost in the thought of his brother Charlie and all the other young men, some of them children that were held hostage in the same place she lays her head every night.

By the time the pair got back to her house it was a little past eleven. "Would you like to come in," Molly asked, in a voice that was a horrible attempt at being flirtatious.

Billy looks up at the window, notices a curtain moving. "Do you have a cat?"

"No, why?"

"It looked like for a moment somebody was in the window." Molly turned around, nervous, "I know I locked the doors."

Billy reaches for the keys in her hands, "I'm going to go and check to make sure that nobody is in there."

"Maybe we should just call the police," but before Molly could finish her sentence, Billy was already opening the door, immerging inside leaving her in the moonlight. She listened carefully, no sound, "Billy," she called out. No response. She quietly stepped inside and finds Billy standing at the doorway between the living room and her bedroom. "Are you okay?"

"Here, it happened here." Molly remained silent. "Sure, you can clean and paint, replace the flooring and tiles, but it is still the same place."

"I thought you never been in here before."

"I remember the news footage. They had footage all over each of the four news channels. Pictures of the scene covered the front page of all the major newspapers, including national. I wonder how long he was here before he got his cronies to bury him in the storage lot that he rented." He turns and looks at Molly, his face ashen, "you know he tore up the concrete in the lot to bury the boys under it. Twenty-three boys they found there. You are going to tell me that nobody heard the commotion of breaking down that concrete. The storage people said they heard or saw nothing." Scratching his beard, "doesn't make sense. somebody had to see that it didn't make sense to be reconstructing a storage room. But nothing, nobody knew nothing. They planted bodies there that they had to put them on top of another until the guy got wise and started taking them down to the beaches of Port Arthur. It completely escapes me as to why those boys didn't say something to someone."

"I was reading today that one of the boys tried to tell his mother that he was involved in killing his friends, but his mom refused to believe it. She didn't call anyone or anything and the other one, well his home life was…"

"Oh, who gives a shit about his homelife! There are plenty of people that come from so called dysfunctional homes. Their parents neglect them or allow them to run amuck, never home or has drugs and guys in and out of the house, but they don't get involved in killing people. It is an excuse that a feeble-minded weakling chose to use to soften the blow that he was a part of a horrendous killing spree. From what I understand, the mother fucker liked it too."

"Billy, sit down. Let me get you something to drink. I don't have any alcohol, but I have…"

"No. I'm sorry, I shouldn't have let this place spook me. I guess all that talk about houses not holding memories was hogwash back at the restaurant." Turning to her, pulling her close, "how about this, Saturday, you come over to my place and I will make you a nice meal. I can cook a hell of a steak, and I promise that I will not be distracted by the ghosts of the past."

"Speaking of ghosts, I guess that you are satisfied nobody is in the house but us."

"Oh, yeah that. I could have sworn somebody was looking out at us, but I guess it was just a trick of the eye. Saturday?"

"That sounds wonderful. I'll bring the wine."

Billy gave her a gentle kiss and she follows him to the door. He turns to give her another peck, and whispers, "keep a light on to scare away from any thrill seekers trying to get a better look at the house." Molly smiled, nodded and closed the door and turns on a lamp visible from the front window illuminating a halo of light while the headlights of cars from the street danced across the living room.

9

Within the Vale

Thump, "Damn speedbumps. Between that and the construction that kid will be rotting before we break ground."

Molly looked around confused of her surroundings. She could feel the wind from the open windows, she could see the streetlights, as they passed by, she could feel how cramped she is in the back of the van, and she could see…Oh my god! Molly swallowed hard, tried to scream out, but no sound would come out of her throat. She tried to move, she thought, if I could just squeeze out and push open the back hatch, but it was no use. A piece of her is trapped in this van with two teen kids, stinking of cigarettes, laughing while one drove and the other chowed down on McDonald's French fries. They don't know I'm here. But how, and where are we going? She drops her hand. and it falls on a heavy plastic bundle. Molly peers closer at it and draws back in disgust. Two glossy blue eyes, stared back at her through the plastic. Motionless but real.

"Can you believe that idiot actually came back to Cory's. Dumb fuck walked right into a trap."

"Why did you kill him? I mean normally Cory does it, but you took over, why?"

"Ah, I don't know. Kid was gonna die anyway. Cory ain't the only badass around here."

Fear shook Molly's spine. Wakeup, Wakeup, Wakeup. She kept pleading to herself.

"It's okay, your safe."

Molly looked over to her side and spots a young frail, thin, young man. He looked just as uncomfortable as she felt as he crouched down near the body, as invisible as she was to the boys in the drivers and passenger seat. "I see this all the time. You get used to it after a while." Molly looks down at the dead boy, sadness overwhelmed her. She feels the van go down a hill, shaking a bit before it came to a complete stop. The driver and the passenger hop out, tussle a bit outside, one arguing with the other to check the surroundings. A short silence and then the back hatch is popped and the moon light sneaks into the van lighting up the plastic bundle which they pull out with an unapologetic clumsiness.

"What are they doing?" Molly whispered to the other invisible passenger.

"No, no need to whisper ma'am. They can't hear us. You see I've tried. Nobody can hear us. We just watch. Come on let's go."

"No," Molly whimpered out not wanting to be a part of the real horror movie playing out before her.

"It's okay, you see, if we ever figure out a way to communicate what we see, we can help their families. I'm still looking for Jeremy and when I figure it out, I'm gonna be a hero!"

He slips out, Molly follows, wearing her night shorts and a tee, no socks. This can't be real, this can't be real, yet no matter how much she tried to deny it, she could feel the wet sand between her toes, the sharp twigs scratch at the bottom of her feet, and the salty night air slapping her skin.

She and her other nightly observer came to a halt as did the other boys. "This will be good here."

"That's Boozer. The one doing most of the digging. He usually does most of the burying and that guy over there," a shaky, icy finger points to a scrawny teen not more than five foot four, "that's Willie. Stay out of his way."

"I thought you said that they can't see us."

"Yeah, but you never know when the vale will be broken."

The pair watched as the two boys began their digging routine. "I bet we could catch some tonight. Smells like rain and the fish always bite during the rain."

"Nah, next time. Cory offered extra if we pick up that Nicholas kid tonight. He's had his eye on him for a while, but

I'm with you. Maybe we can come back later and pull the boat out and catch us some before morning."

Molly shuttered at the casual manner of the conversation. "I can't stand to watch this?" Molly whispered.

"Then don't but at least try to remember this spot. This exact spot that way if you are ever able to tell someone where he is at you can."

"Where who is at?"

"Gracin, that's his name. Gracin." His mom and dad are probably worried about him unless he's been gone so long, they forgot him. They need to know where Gracin is at." He then looks directly at her. His features young, soft and kind. "Peter is over there, and Mark and Carlos are over there." Turning back to the scene, "I don't remember things to good and they get worse and worse, but I make it a point to remember their names and where they are at so if I am ever able to tell, I will. Cuz nobody deserves to be forgotten but if they are gone to long, they get forgotten."

"No, they don't." Molly crosses her arms to shield for the night chill which keeps tasting her skin. "They don't ever forget."

"I hope so." He turned towards the two boys who were walking back up to the van with their shovels. "They are going to go and pick up more friends for Cory. That's why they didn't drink all the beer. They are using it to bribe people to be Cory's friends."

“I don't want to watch this.”

“Then wake up.”

10

2001

Molly's eyes snapped open. The alarm clock ringing, "Shit!" she shouts. Jumping out of bed, she slips and notices her feet. They are dirty, even with a wild grass vine wrapped around her right big toe. "What the hell," she pulls herself up, picks up her covers and notices the sheets are filthy and damp. Quickly she rips the sheets off and goes to the laundry room adjacent to the kitchen. On the counter she sees one of her steak knives out, just lying there. She states at it squinting her eyes. I haven't used those in weeks.

She then goes to take a shower, needing a little bit of extra time to scrub out an extra layer of sand that clung to her scalp. Weird. This is too weird!

After completing her shower, she throws on some leggings and a tee-shirt and begins to scour the Internet. Cory Dennison's crimes. Cory Dennison's burial sites. Cory Dennison's van. Cory Dennison's victims. Anything Cory Dennison. Pictures upon pictures pop up. The ones of the van were not too clear though. What she could see, looked like that there were wooden boxes, makeshift coffins perhaps in the back of it. She did not remember any of that from her dream. She also did not remember the torture objects as it was described in the mobile sex torture van. But what she did remember was that it was white, there were not any seats in the back and that her and another dream visitor were in the back, a dead body nestled between them.

11

The Pied Piper's Prince

I don't know what kind of spell that Cory has over those boys, but it is starting to get scary. I've lost count how many friends that were brought to him. I stand around, I pace, I try to knock things over, anything to be a distraction, something to get Cory's attention or Willie or Boozer's. Nothing works. They are too focused. I whisper to the boys that it is going to be all right. I know it is a lie, and mom said I should never lie. I want to bring them comfort, anything to help them in their moments of terror. It doesn't matter anyway. They never seem to hear me. Some try to fight back, but they can't. Others just give in. They are strapped down; only able to twist and wiggle. Not match for Cory. Never a fair fight. Even though Cory is huge in stature, he still has them strapped down. Pinned like a helpless chicken waiting for the slaughter. Most of the time he strangles them. Willie, he's smaller so he shoots them with Cory's gun. He likes that. The boys never have a chance.

But I am going to help them somehow. Maybe not them directly but I am going to help their families. You see, if I can get all their secrets, and then find a way to give them to the police. That can help the families. Maybe then, I can go home to Ralph and Mom. So far, I have counted three sites where Willie and Boozer take the boys after Cory is done with them. The 24-Hour public storage shed, a lake that is a little while a way and the beaches of Port Arthur. It's random, where they choose the boys' resting place. I guess it is up to whatever Willie wants to do with them. Boozer just goes along. Boozer likes to try and please everyone. I can relate to that.

So, I follow along unnoticed. Like a shadow. I work to erase the fog so I can remember every road, every path and even logs that could lead to where the boys are. That way they can be found. I don't know how long I have been doing this. Seen a lot of sunrises and sunsets so they all start to blur together. I never know the season either. Never seen a Christmas tree in the places that Cory occupies or even a talk of any kind of celebration. Just Halloween, but I've learned to flicker the lights enough in hopes that children will stay away. Teens like to go trick or treating too you know. But I don't want them to come to Cory's. He may like them. You know, like them the way he likes me and want to keep them around, or he may just want them for a temporary playmate, but they still won't get to go home anytime soon. That is why I have to keep watch and follow. I'm gonna be a hero someday. Benny says if you say something enough times, it will happen. That is what I am doing. I'm gonna make it happen.

12

Within the Vale

"Come join in on the party," Willie says in a friendly voice. Like he was for real, he wanted to hang out with Tommy. He even invited Tammy, Tommy's friend who was thinking of running away on account of her stepdad's temper.

"Run, Run, Run."

"What's happening?" Molly whispers looking around again. "This looks different."

"Sometimes we bounce."

"What do you mean, we bounce?" Now growing accustomed to her dream companion.

"We see things happening at different times but not necessary in order." Then looking at the teens. "That's Tommy and Tammy. Cory only wanted Tommy to come over, but Willie felt bad because she wanted to get away from home and away from her stepdad. Course she's never seen a temper like that of Cory. I've seen Cory get mad, even when he thought nobody was watching. But somebody is always watching. Sometimes I think it is the devil himself, poking at him. Trying to get him mad. When I see Cory strangle those boys, I swear I hear a wicked laugh vibrating through the house. Cory, Willie and Boozer, they don't hear it, but I do, and I know it is pure evil."

"Is he going to kill them?"

"Eventually. Maybe not right now but the playmates always die. That's the game. They have to die because it is part of the game."

Molly shudders, geez, I wonder if I am talking in my sleep. "Only pure evil causes a person to call people you know; that trust you to come over to party, be there friend, only to leave them to a malicious torture and death."

"What's worse is I think Willie may have like Tammy too. Look how pretty she is."

Molly examines the girl for a moment. Long blonde hair and dark eyes slender frame. She smiled at Willie exposing perfect teethe. "I think I would have liked to date someone like Tammy." Molly barely heard her dream escort as Cory stomps through the house.

"Cory's not happy about Tammy being here. I think he likes Tommy all right. I mean, Tommy wasn't normally his type seeing how he had dark hair and a tan. He likes guys like me with light hair and light eyes. Tall but not strong. He never wants anyone to be stronger than him."

The two watch Cory as he grabs Willie by the collar and yells, "I don't want no girl hanging out here. Girls are nothing but trouble and drama."

Willie panics, "Look, her dad kicked her out. She has nowhere to go and besides, she's hot. Can't I have someone to play with once in a while? Besides, look at her, she's gonna be out in no time and then you can have your fun."

Cory seemed to calm down at that and goes out to the living room, tossing a few beers at the kids, the girl missing hers tumbled to the floor beside her. Cory snorts and pulls out a box of weed and papers. Tommy and Tammy hadn't tried the stuff before stared at him wide-eyed. Stupid fools. Drugs are bad. They should listen to their moms not some stranger they just met. Molly thought with a panicked urgency.

Willie smoked and drank with them while making small talk. Cory sat back observing with an angry stare, waiting until the three passed out.

"That's his MO, you know." David whispers to Molly as she watches the scene unfold.

"What a coward."

"I don't follow."

"Stupid piece of shit is such a huge guy, and yet he lets drugs and booze weaken their reflexes so he can subdue them easier. Won't even let them have a chance to fight. What a puss."

The two stood quietly as they watched Cory gag and strap his prey to the torture boards handcuffing their wrists through the knot holes.

This time, strapping Willie too. "Ha! I've seen this part before." David leans in narrating the scene for Molly. "Wait for it. Willie is about to open his eyes and throw a fit when he sees his fate is lying in the hands of this mad man."

Molly blinked her eyes, partly hoping to wake up, but part of her wanted to see the final scene in this real-life horror story. As Willie realizes he is being betrayed while getting bound so tight that he could barely flip his head to see his two new pieces of prey strapped on boards next to him as if they were the appetizers and he was the main course.

"What they hell Cory," Willie yells out flabbergasted terror.

"Mother always said, you play with a rattlesnake, not matter what you do for them, you'll eventually will get bit." Molly murmured. "I guess Willie got bit."

I don't think you could call Cory a rattlesnake. Too kind of a word for that even though they are the most feared snake in this part of Texas." As David spoke, he never broke his gaze. "Cory is more like a demon."

"Do you believe in demons?" Molly asked hesitantly.

"Watch this." Molly turns his head back to the scene, Cory's voice roared to a sound that that most would consider unhuman, his nostrils flaring and the look in his eyes gleamed into a monstrous glow.

"This is usually when I leave." David said. "Not always deliberate too. Sometimes I find myself in the living room, looking out that front window, hoping somebody will see me. Somehow my voice will break through the glass barrier and one of those people on the street will hear my shrieks or those of Cory's friends. Somebody will figure out that something is not right, and they will come in and rescue us all. This time," David shrugs his shoulders "This time it is Willie that needs rescuing which has got to have surprised the crap out of him."

Upon Cory realizing that Willie is awake, he yanks off his gag and spits in his face, "thought it was a good idea to bring the girl over did ya, well now you gonna die cuz of her."

Willie pleads with Cory. "I told ya, I had to bring her, it was the only way to get Tommy here and you said you wanted Tommy. You pointed him out the other day when we went to get burgers. Sides, you ain't gotta worry about her, I'll take care of her."

Cory stands up, snarling but Willie keeps insisting "I'll take care of them both. You don't gotta do nothing but have your fun with Tommy. Let me go and I'll take care of Tammy now."

Cory pauses, he grabs Willie's crouch, "you better not be fucking with me kid." He then uncuffs Willie.

Willie, rubs his wrists, "I won't let you down."

David turns to Molly, "I gotta admit, the first time I saw this play out, I was disappointed. I mean, if he got rid of Willie, maybe he wouldn't have anyone to bring him friends and the end of this nightmare would be over, and I could go home to Mom and Ralph." Looking down at his feet, "that is, if they haven't forgotten me."

13

2001

Molly blinked and smiled, only catching a fraction of what Mrs. Madison was saying about her husband and his last moments before the explosion. Catching herself when the sweet lady asked her if she is alright, she simply nods and resigns herself to focus on the chemical fire that stole Mr. Madison's life. This was big news; Hopefully, I can find enough research to fill in the blanks. Then recalculating her brain, she focused on what she did catch from the one-way conversation. Mr. Madison was a foreman and had gone thirty-three days accident free before the explosion happened. It is the same story heard written in papers all around the surrounded communities that had industry that revolved around the Ship Channel. Middle-aged man, working to support his soccer mom wife and two daughters and then Bam, an explosion, random or maybe not, that took out twenty workers at once, her husband being one of them. It was better than her usual story and she was thankful of the opportunity, but the air in this lady's living room was as depressing as it probably was the day that it happened.

"I couldn't get off the couch for about three months. Went to work for one of those temp agencies, could only land jobs that earned eight dollars an hour. Can't make a living off eight dollars an hour, especially when the only skills you have is hosting a bake sale for the school PTA."

Molly leans over to the left and sees a young girl peeking out. She smiles and offers a hello. "Ashley, Ashley Darlene, what are you doing hiding about there. Mrs. Madison turns to her as if she had something to apologize for. "So sorry, Ms. Matthews, she's never been around a real writer."

"Well, I'm nothing to brag about." Molly's imposter syndrome always had a hard time accepting the idea of her being a real writer. Most of the time she felt like a little girl playing reporter make-believe.

"Oh, I've read your book River's Bend. I think it is something to brag about. Course I wouldn't let my girls read it. The oldest is only thirteen and well, you" she puts her hand to the side of her mouth, but her voice is too loud to shield any words, "you tend to write about sex a lot." Molly swallows hard in embarrassment but keeps her composure.

"I've got enough here Ms. Madison, I'll give you a call when the story prints and again, congratulations on the settlement. I hope it helps you out with the girls." Mrs. Madison smiled and followed her as Molly got up to walk to the door. Molly knew she really didn't have enough but she also knew that Eddie wouldn't care as long as she gave him a thousand words and an upbeat story on how the widow was going to be just fine and what an upstanding Christian she is.

She sits in her car for a moment feeling the Texas heat knocking at the window. Urging the realization that she is less than two blocks away from the Southwest Public Storage. Burial grounds. One of many Dennison's cemeteries. An unusual resting spot. I wonder how many times Dennison visited them relishing in his own personal corpse dump site. She shivered; I can't do this. Just get out of your lease as soon as you can. God knows I have reason. Asshole should have told me what happened in the house. Like always though, her morbid curiosity did the thinking for and in this case the driving as she turns her car to the direction of the storage shed.

She stared at it for the longest time from the parking lot. The once quaint name of Golden Rise Street now changed to East Harvard Street in efforts to escape the past. How naïve of government officials to think that crime watch seekers wouldn't figure out that the street name was changed. What had not change was the storage shed. There it was in all of its glory. Red and white dingy paint restored a few times to the original horror, yet it still looked like a run-down ratty hide-away storage shed. To a normal observer, it would look like any other run-down betrayal of restoration gone bad east of Houston. She wasn't sure how long she had been looking at it when a friendly elderly lady came out asking, "Can I help you with something dear?"

Crap, this looks bad. What am I gonna say? "Uhm, yeah, I was wondering what the largest shed you have?"

"Well, we got some as big as 50 by 60. Can fit a lot of stuff in there. You looking to store your furniture until you get your own place? That's why most people get those. To hide the assets until the dust settles."

"Huh what?"

"Hide your furniture. Is that why you need it. Going through a messy divorce. Such a crying shame how couples can't work out their differences." Molly looked at her confused.

"Come on dear. I'll show you around."

At this point, Molly felt since of obligation to see this out so with little hesitation, she relented to the manager's story about going through a bad breakup and needing a place to store her stuff temporarily until she got back on her feet. Gladys she would soon find out was her name, didn't ask her for a driver's license or anything. Just walked her right into the place. Still faintly recognizable from the ancient news footage from 1973. Much better now. Or at least much cleaner. The storage units felt like a maze. A rat looking for cheese except there isn't any cheese. There's blood, a trail of it and no amount of new cement or layers of paint is going to erase the hidden evil of this place. Much like the place that I am disgusted to call home.

Molly asked, "How long has this place been here?"

"Ah, hell, I don't know. I didn't ask may questions when I took the job. Needed the work and this is where I found it." Molly kept trying to follow the woman's brisk pace but suddenly she became nauseous, and a streak of pain stung her exactly between the eyes. "You okay," the woman notices her swooning reaching to grasp for nothing but there was nothing to grasp.

"Uhm, I think I need to sit down," Molly stumbles and leans on the side of a shed while the lady helps her. She couldn't hear what she was saying though as sound blurred and for a moment she was in a silent fog where words became inaudible and even the traffic rushing by became distant whooshes. Through blurred vision she makes out the silhouette of the young man she kept seeing in her dreams.

"Does he work here," she points to an empty space only filled with blue sky and a row of more storage sheds.

"Who dear? I don't see anybody." The lady said looking ahead, "I'm the only one working, it's just me and two other employees but we take shifts, one at a time. You probably saw another renter. He's gone now. Renters come and go as they please. If they pay their rent, we don't pay them any mind."

Yeah, how convenient for serial killers. Molly's heart started to beat faster, her mouth prickling dry, her head spinning, "I think I should go." Then remembering her lie, "I'll come back if I decide to proceed with my plans," coming across as another wish-washy unhappy housewife looking to find herself. Gladys firmly asking her is she was okay to drive.

Molly went straight home after her visit to the storage shed. Her plan, write her article, get it to Eddie, collect two hundred dollars and work on her pathetic romance novel that will only be sold to horny storage shed renters while she figured her next plan of action. Instead, she went straight home, took a shower, feeling better, ate some left-over KFC not clear on exactly how old it was, drank a coke and then went and laid down. Daylight still busting through the window she collapses into a tense slumber only to be wakened a short time later by a rustling in her living room.

She laid there staring up at the ceiling fan enveloped by darkness, she blinked, but for a moment, which was the only thing she could do. Paralyzed from the neck down her eyes shifted to the side when a loud thud sounds into the room accompanied by two men arguing and struggling to drag two unconscious teens, a boy and a girl. "Here, grab the cuffs, and hook em up to the board." The older tall man growled at his younger accomplice. "Here's knife, cut that bitch's clothes off, you can rape her and then get rid of her. I got him."

Molly's reoccurring companion walked up to her.

"Why am I seeing this again?"

"We bounced back," David whispered.

"You see it happening. Do something. Something has to be done. He does this over and over again." As he spoke the big man's voice snarled above his in a wicked sneer.

"You shouldn't have brought that bitch here. I told you, no girls. Now, you've done fucked things up. I should kill you too Willie for being the no-good screw up that you are. The two others, now stripped and cuffed to the plywood had woken up. Tommy began to cry, Tammy screeching, "Is this for real?"

"Yes," Willie hollers with irritation.

" What are you going to do anything about it?" Tammy cried out. Too much in disbelief to allow the fear to sink in.

Molly's friend zooms over to Willie. "She's right," he said in a panic, "she's right. You could do something about this right now. You could make it stop. Make it stop!"

14

The Pied Piper's Prince

I never really understood hunting. I know in Texas there is a season for it, and it is a macho thing to do. Lure in your prey, kill it and eat it. Yet, it never made any sense to me. Not when there is a Piggly Wiggly down the street. Besides, it's not a fair fight when bullets, or strength or dominance is involved. There is no way to even out the playing field with an animal. When I was in school, I had to read a story by Richard Connell called The Most Dangerous Game. It was about these two guys that like to hunt for sport. Not to eat to survive but to play for trophies. Except one of the characters played for human trophies, putting the other in a situation where he had to outsmart the other to survive. I found the concept fascinating and sad at the same time. I talked to Mom about it, and she said that was the nature of primitive man. Kill or be killed. Maybe not as literal as that, but I know that Mom was always struggling to make ends meet as she would say after my dad left. She was always scrambling, but she never hurt nobody, much more kill somebody. She lives, like we all do, struggling to survive for the moment but dream for the future. Only, Rainsford had already accomplished his dream and his role was reversed while Zaroff chased his dream and that the moment of the story, which was taking down Rainsford.

Mom's story isn't the same. I mean, it wasn't like somebody was going after her with a rifle and she had to create a tiger trap or something, but the way she put it was that life is a game and that there are hunters of different types and that I needed to know and learn about the best choices. Hunt for a job, to make a comfortable living for myself and anyone that I may choose to share my life with. Next step, hunt for the person that I want to share my life with but whatever I use to lure them with, I need to be consistent and keep up with it. Girls may like bad boys for a while, Mom says, but what they want in a good man is stability. She said, you don't just treat a girl good while courting her, you are to treat her good even after the capture. Flowers and candy should not be bait, it should be the expectation as to what is to come.

I told her that flowers are sometimes expensive, and people get mad when you pick them out of their gardens. She told me to never be a rat. I asked her to explain, and she said that cheese is put in traps to catch mice and rats. It lures them because they like cheese, and they think they are getting a reward when they approach the trap but instead, once they take a bite, the trap shuts down on them and kills them. Just like that. They are slaughtered.

I told her that I wasn't a rat, and I won't get trapped. Mom said that we are all rats, just the circumstances change but that we will all get trapped at some point and we need to be able to recognize it. We can always escape if we try hard enough.

I guess that I am trapped now, cuz I keep trying to get away from the cycle of trips that I follow Cory and his friends on, but I can never get away. Sometimes I think, Cory can see me, and he is happy that I am here cuz he knows that I am trapped. That I am a rat, and he no longer needs cheese to keep me.

15

2001

"Billy, I really think there is something in my house."

"Well, I can understand that the circumstances, and the history of the place will make you think so. It is also understandable that you are having some bad dreams. When did you say your lease is up?"

"I know I sound crazy, but I was awake when I saw what I saw."

Billy looks at her intently, "you are welcome to stay here if you don't feel safe, I imagine you get a lot of pranksters bothering you at night."

"I can't hide from my own house. If what I am seeing is not real, then I'm crazy, if it is real and then it's not and," Molly sighs in frustration, "or least…I mean, I don't know how to describe it. It is like I am seeing into the house's memory. Stupid, the city should have knocked that place down when the story broke out. I've heard of other cases when something horrific has happened in a location and the city tears it down, why leave this house?"

"I can't answer any of that, just like I can't fully explain your hallucinations."

"They're not hallucination. I'm telling you, what I see and hear is real."

"Well, I've heard where a place, any place can have a residual effect. I have even heard of residual hauntings. Not sure if I agree with that kind of notion but it could be possible. Especially with the things that went on there."

"I am not sure what you mean."

"Well, like you said, it was like you are seeing the house's memory. Maybe you are."

"A house is an object, not an idea. There is no possible way that I can be seeing in the past."

"No but you are experiencing echoes of events as to what has happened there." Nodding his head, "I don't think you are crazy."

"That's good to know. But how do I stop experiencing these so-called echoes without some heavy medication."

"Well, like I said about residual hauntings. Echoes of memories are like a haunting. So, it would seem fit to call in a team for a paranormal investigation."

"You mean like the Warren's."

"Well, yeah, but I'd imagine that you couldn't just pick up the phone and go hey, Ed and Lorraine, can you hop on a plane down to Houston and get rid of some bad vibes in my rent house that I plan to move out of in a matter of a few months." Seeing Molly's frustration Billy's voice softens, "Nah you may be able to find a local psychic medium or someone like that who has dealt with this kind of stuff."

"I don't think I believe in such things."

"I get it, and I don't blame you for being a little weary but there are some good ones out there that may be able to help."

"Yeah, there are also some that are smart enough to type in 2020 Winkle Street in the computer and find out the whole grisly history of the house and create a so-called cold reading out of that."

"True, but the trick is, tell them as little as possible to what you are experiencing to see if they are the real deal, then when they show up and they start giving you some cold bullshit psychobabble, you can pick up on it quickly."

"I don't know. I mean, I wouldn't even know how to begin to look for one."

"Well, it is still early, let's drive down to Galveston. There is a lady who works out of one of those occult bookstores who claims to be able to do readings. We can give her a try and if she seems like the real deal, maybe we could get her to do a reading at the house."

"It is a pretty night; I could go for a drive to the beach. Are you sure she will be working?"

"It's a weekend, she is always there on the weekend."

"So how do you know about her."

"Well, if I tell you that you will think that I am crazy." Billy waited for a laugh and when he didn't get one, he finally said, "Look, I know that it may seem like nonsense but when Charlie disappeared my mother called in a whole line of psychics. She was desperate you know." Grabbing his keys. "Anyway, there were a few that did seem to hold some talents. It's just the answers my mom got were ones that she didn't like."

Following Billy out to the car, "why, what were the answers?"

"That he was in a cold dark, wet place." Stating more to himself than to her, "he was one of the bodies that was recovered on the beach. One of those hoodlums wrapped him up in industrial plastic but they did a shit job in tying it up and water leaked in, rotting most of his features. He was unrecognizable when they found him. Had to use dental records. If Charlie didn't have a lot of cavities, who knows if we would have ever been able to bury him. He would probably still be in pieces in a box in some crime lab."

"That's awful. You know we don't have to do this. I know it must hurt, bringing up these awful memories. I can understand if you want to close that door to your life."

"That door will never be closed. When something like that happens to your family, someone you know and love, it will never go away into some dark place tucked up into a container of distant memories. Maybe partly, but there is always a crack of it, propped open, begging for you to discover the truth. Nobody can let go of something like that."

"But you have had some closure. You know what happened to him and the monster who did it is dead."

"Yes, but I don't know why. Was my brother a random selection or was he somebody that Dennison picked out, to lure into his torture chamber before killing him. I will also always wonder if I would eventually been led to that same trap. How Dennison got those young boys to do his bidding has always baffled me. He trained them to pull in other boys, like Charlie knowing what he was going to do them. Some of these boys was his friend. Hell, Charlie went to elementary school with that Willie guy."

"Willie?"

"Yeah, that's one of his flunkies."

"Willie is one of the names I heard in last night's vision. He was one of the people committing the acts."

"He is still alive isn't he."

"So, a haunting does not explain what I saw."

"But it is not Willie doing the haunting. It is the house, and the memories burned into the foundation that is harboring all this evil. Maybe it is too much for the house. Maybe, like how a person needs to confess their sins, maybe a house needs to confess the sins it sheltered, and you are the only one available to listen."

"Maybe we should ask the psychic to do a cleansing."

"Maybe. Or maybe you are right. The damn place just needs to be torn down."

16

Pied Piper's Prince

The beach, the forest, the storage unit. They are running out of places. That's good. If there are not any places to hide the remains, then why kill? No place to put them.

Doesn't matter, Cory is responsible in other areas in his life. He has a girlfriend that he even introduced to Willie and Boozer. He mows his lawn, goes to work, makes up his bed even, and he pays his bills. On the surface he is a perfectly normal man, with a normal job, a normal girlfriend and yet; he is now on a waiting list to get another boat shed. I think he is hoping to get one near the first one he is renting. Nobody there questions him. I mean, wouldn't you think it suspicious that someone wants another shed when the one they already have appeared empty. Well, not above ground that is.

This is not good, not good, not good. There are always boys, there are always hiding places. Boozer seems tired of this. It all seems to be getting to him. He is making these mutterings about how he doesn't want to do this anymore. If he can have a conscience than Willie and Cory could have one too. If Boozer could just persuade Willie, maybe they can end this.

They could be free. They wouldn't have to capture anyone anymore. Then, I could be free. I miss Ralph. I miss Mom.

17

2001

"Hi, I'm Sharon," The psychic raised her hand to shake Molly's. She was a heavy-set woman, about the same height of Molly, shoulder length hair that couldn't decide if it wanted to stay blonde or turn white, black straight skirt, black blouse with tiny polka dots with ruffles around the wrists and the neck. What, no exotic name, dark clothes, dark polish on the nails, heavy makeup. She looks like a 1970's housewife for God's sake.

Sharon leads Billy and Molly through the bookstore filled with magical type trinkets, used books, goth jewelry and an assortment of candles and oils. She pulls aside a set of beads hanging from a doorway, resembling a groovy hipster show where everyone has long hair, smokes dope and wears lots of bracelets, short skirts or flared jeans. Everyone except for Sharon. She looked normal. Perfectly normal. Almost scary normal. Of course, so did Ted Bundy.

"So," Sharon chirps while shuffling a deck of Tarot cards. "Am I doing a couple's reading?"

"No not exactly," as Molly spoke, Sharon's eyes narrows and she says softly, "You have a spirit reaching out for you."

"You can see him," Molly says shakily, looking all around her.

"No, he's not here now, but I can feel him. He's reaching out for help."

Molly's attention turns to Billy. "Don't look at me, I didn't tell her nothing. I just told the guy upfront that we wanted a reading." Molly turns back to face Sharon.

"Go on."

"Don't worry, he is not a negative entity. I know it is hard to believe, hauntings and all, but not all spirits are bad. In fact, I think this one may believe that he is protecting you."

"You said, he was reaching out for help."

"Ahh yes, he is. He doesn't know that he is able to leave. He thinks he must do something. That if he doesn't something terrible will happen."

"Like unresolved business. That's why a ghost stays right, they have unresolved business."

"I don't think that is the case here. I mean, maybe he thinks he has unresolved business, but he was taken care of years ago. He feels that he needs to fulfill a purpose and maybe somehow you are part of that purpose."

Molly turns to Billy. "This is too vague. I need direct clear-cut answers on how to get this thing out of my house."

Sharon takes a breath and then looks at her intently. "There is more than one spirit." Molly looks back at her, Sharon continues. "I know that you think you need this spirit out of your house, and he does need to depart, but once he leaves, you are going to have another whole can of worms to deal with."

Molly, not fully listening, huffs, "one thing at a time. If I can get rid of this guy and the other mess that is in there doesn't contact me than I should be okay."

"Be careful what you wish for," Sharon warns. "You see, right now, this spirit that is reaching out for you, he is an active barrier between you and what else is tucked away hidden in your house. If you are not careful, there is no telling what you might awaken." Sharon gets up, "here, let's put together the things that you need to cleanse your house and that will help some but not completely."

"What do you mean?"

"There is more to your story, I can feel it. More to your ghost story if it is indeed a ghost."

"But you said that there was nothing negative about him."

"No, he is not a negative entity at all, but he is surrounded by negativity and great evil and that leads you vulnerable to that evil. It feels to me as if demons are haunting your ghost and if he escapes or goes away well than, they will come after you.”

“Oh, great, the haunting is being haunted. I don’t do well with riddles.”

“I am afraid this is far more sinister than a riddle. Is it your home that you picked up this spirit?”

“She lives in a murder house,” Billy piped in impatiently. “We think she is having visions of the past.”

“Oh, that makes sense.” Sharon pursed her lips together.

“What makes sense?”

“You live in a traumatized home. It makes sense that it would need to be cleansed.”

“Well now I have heard it all. Everyone needs therapy these days. There are people that are taking their pets to therapy for Christ’s sake. Now you are telling me my home, an actual object is traumatized. It is a house. Houses don’t have feelings.”

Sharon comes closer to Molly and in a gentle voice, “I can’t imagine how difficult this must be for you. It sounds like you are having to live the history of things that occurred long before your time. I apologize if I came across as insensitive, but I must encourage you, to cleanse your home. It may not solve the problem entirely but at least it will send the message that you are taking action against whatever this is.”

"So will you come, and do it?" Molly shrugged her shoulders, "we'll pay of course."

"I will help you get the materials," Sharon is shaking her head, "and I can put together some prayers, but as for the cleansing of your home, you will have to do it yourself." Giving Molly a pleasant smile, "dear, it doesn't want me there, and I don't think that I am strong enough to take it on. But you my dear, faith will bring you strength. I am also going to give you a protection spell or prayer so to speak as well, and I want you to wear a rose quartz around your neck. Do you have a blue-tiger-eye ring or any tiger eye jewelry for that matter?"

"I don't think I can do that. I mean, the evil energy, well the killer, it was his house. He got it from his father. He spent some of his own teen years there. For all I know that is where his tormented thoughts of violence first began."

"That is why it is so important that you stand your ground. You take charge of the home, not just with your intellect but with your heart and soul."

"You don't think that monster wants to eat me alive?"

"I know it does." Sharon rustled through the store, grabbing candles and sage. "The sage is for the initial cleansing, but the white candles must be lit for nine days straight in a row. Let them burn out all night. Don't let them go out on their own. You must keep one in each room of the house." She then quickly writes chants on a piece of paper.

"So now you are making me a witch or something. Should I get a cauldron too." Billy shook his head and reached for the supplies.

"I am very sorry Sharon. She's extremely stressed. This is a lot to take in."

Sharon's voice was calm and kind, "this is a lot for anyone, and I know you want to help, but this is her fight. She must be willing to do this on her own. I'm afraid there may be more at stake than human spirits and she must stand her ground."

The couple were quiet on the car ride back from Galveston. When they finally arrived at Billy's he urgently began to persuade her to stay. "You can stay in the spare bedroom, no funny business I promise. Go back during the daylight."

"Billy, thank you so much, for everything." Looking at her car, "especially for believing me. You are a special kind of person. Most people would just have passed me off as crazy."

"You're not crazy, and I am very much worried about you."

"Don't be. This is my battle."

"Warrior Princess Molly!"

"Something like that."

18

The Pied Piper's Prince

Cory did know how to throw a party. Decked out the whole front of his place like a teenage game room. A pool table, fridge full of beers and wrap around couches, which were comfortable to lay back in. He always had weed in the house and all the other sinful comforts. He was smart about it too. He would collect the keys of his visitors, he said it was for safety reasons convincing them that he didn't want anybody drinking and then driving after leaving his house, but that didn't make a bit of sense because they never drove themselves, and yet, not only was he able to get his guests keys but other personal items such as wallets and ID cards."

The bedrooms of his house aren't as attractive. Often the floor was carpeted with large pieces of thick industrial plastic, the sheets were stained and never changed out, plyboards leaned up against the walls, ashtrays littered the nightstand and thick heavy drapes covered the window. He also had a strange assortment of sex toys, magazines that displayed bondage on the covers and odd-looking belts and whips.

The first time I was there, I could not take in the scenery because I was overwhelmed by the smell. It smelled like urine even though I don't think that Cory was that animalistic but maybe his friends were. I don't recall him ever letting them loose to take care of their personal business. Maybe he thought that they would run away or something but that would have been difficult as he keeps bolts on all the doors and only has lights on when it is necessary.

19

2001

Molly took a deep breath before she turned the key to unlock her house. It was late now, much later than when she usually came home, she was tired and relieved. Relieved that Billy believed her and relieved that he was willing to come the next day to help with the house, even though Sharon told him directly to stay out of it.

As soon as she stepped inside the threshold, she heard a noise. A clunking sound like two pool balls hitting each other. She turned on the light, but it flickered, so she reached for the lamp. Her initial thought, run, get back in your car, go directly to Billy's and never come back. Instead, she edged toward the noise. It was then that she saw the shadow of a man, over six feet tall leaning over a pool table, hitting the balls knocking two in one.

straightening himself up, he leans against his cue stick, Molly clutching her bag of cleansing contents close to her, but remembering Sharon's words, she stands her ground.

"You need to leave."

The penumbra of a man or beast, Molly wasn't sure, laughed, laughed so hard, the sound vibrated through the house. "You think you can make me leave. You've got prayers and chants with a few candles. Don't mess with me bitch. I've got the devil on my side. Besides, I'm not even sure if you believe in god, you snivel snit."

And with that, the pool table, the cue sticks, and the thing faded, leaving her alone in the moonlight of the living room.

20

Within the Vale

"He's got to do something; he's got to do something." The boy was pleading at Molly. "Make him do something."

Molly squinted, she tried to speak but nothing would come out. This isn't real, this isn't real, running through her mind, yet the coldness beside her chilled every bone in her body while a heat bubbled inside her head, and the shrieking, crying teens evaporated into the depths of her heart, trembled tears leaking out of her eyes.

"I don't want to die, do something!" Tommy screamed out as Cory violently prodded him with the end of a mop handle, laughing in a whooping hollering kind of way, the boy's anguish sounds muffled by loud music blaring in the living room, going to have a funk good time, the JBs wailed.

"Make them stop, make them stop!"

"I can't" Molly said through gritted teeth, tears streaming out harder now, this isn't real, this isn't real." Molly didn't know if she was muttering, speaking out loud or praying, but another voice came through.

"Willie are you fucking kidding me. Is this for real?"

"Yeah, it's for real," Willie huffed, fumbling with her pants. "Damn girl these are tight."

"Well, what are you going to do about it?"

Wille shouts at Cory while dragging Tammy, still attached to the torture board, "I'm gonna take this bitch to another room."

"Why are we seeing this again?" Molly stammered out. "We've seen this scene over and over again. Why?"

"I don't really know. But somehow it is important to us getting out."

"What do you mean us. You're the one stuck here." David looks at Molly confused but then turns back to the scene. Cory ignoring Willie at placing his attention on Tommy. Willie stops in his tracks as somehow; he felt his eyes forced to lock with those of Tommy's. Tammy's words darting into his ears stinging his mind.

"That's your friend in their damnit." Then through a sniffle, "I'm your friend," Willie hesitates. "We wouldn't be here if you hadn't brought us. Why Wille, why? Why would you do this do us?"

"Do something," Molly ghostly friend whimpers.

A surge of sore rage buckles in Molly, her fear paralysis subsides as she pulls herself up in the bed, stares straight out in the scene and gurgles a bellowing shout, "Do Something!"

21

2001

Molly drenched in sweat sit up in bed and wipes the beads dripping from her forehead. The shadows gone, the morning light streaming in through the curtains, her nightgown sticking to her body, her nose twitching at the smell of old blood lingering in the air. The morning birds singing outside oblivious to the haunting terror within the walls.

She glances around her, feels a cramp, and looks down and gasps in disgust. She is sitting in a patch of a red sticky stain, some sticking between her legs. She tries to jump up but nearly falls due to the stiffness of her body not yet recovered from the recent night terrors. Breathing in and out, she manages to relax until her jerky movements become accompanied by the aching cramps of her menstrual cycle. She pulls the sheets off the bed, her nightshirt off and pads to the washing machine in just her socks, leaving a smudged trail of blood. Gross, wiping what she could with her sock, she goes to the shower and lets the water run over her for half an hour.

Her body sore, her mind spinning, she is only beckoned out of the shower with the sound of her cell phone chiming. She checks, a missed call from her mom, one from Eddie and three from Billy.

"Well Eddie brings in the paycheck, so I guess I will call him first."

"You interview Mrs. Madison yesterday."

"Yeah, I sure did, plan on writing the article this morning and bringing it to you first thing tomorrow. Why you call on a Sunday anyway."

"Mrs. Madison died yesterday."

"Wait what? She was as fit as a fiddle when I left her."

"Only telling you what I know. Her sister called the paper bright and early stating that around five last night she had a heart attack or something. One of her daughters found her and called her aunt all hysterical. Nobody knows quite what it was but apparently, she died on the spot. Guess she didn't stand a chance."

"So, I take if you want me to scrap the article?"

"No, not exactly, I want you to do one of those romance pieces like you do for your books except without the sex stuff. You know, turn it into a loss piece as to how she couldn't live without her man and that even with the settlement, all she wanted was him. You know, some crap like that. I think I can brand that better."

"So let me get this straight; even though she lived on for a year, you want to exploit this lady's death to gain notoriety for the paper even though she is leaving behind two young daughters. You sure that is going to sit well considering they have suddenly become orphaned?"

"Hun, we have been losing sales for a long time. Thanks to your kid's digital media whatever it is, papers are on the out. Got have some kind of gimmick before I am completely out of business. But if you must, tie in some sweet piece about her kids. Who knows, it may bring in donations for them or something. Everybody needs a leg up once in a while."

"Well, I can't even imagine that, but your take does make this easier to write."

"That a girl." As Eddie was speaking, Billy was calling in.

"I gotta go, but I can make it happen. When do you want it by?"

"Hate to ask you to work on a Sunday,"

"But you're asking right?", before he could respond, Molly, said, "no problem. I see what I can do." She then hung up, while ignoring Billy's call to put on some pajama shorts and a tee shirt, and a fresh pair of socks.

Molly spent the better part of the morning pounding away at her keyboard. The story came easy to her. Mr. Madison was in the Navy when she met his beloved. By the time she was done with romancing their meeting and their happy life together, she was 2500 words in and realized she had something better here than the plot of her current work in progress. Damn, maybe they should be my main characters.

While she was proofreading her piece, a knock sounded at the door. She looked up, it was already three and she hadn't eaten or put on suitable clothing. She looks up and she sees Billy's red Dodge parked out front. Crap, she didn't want him there, but he did do lot for her, more than she can even imagine and she didn't bother to call him back.

"Sorry, I've been working all morning. I am not even dressed.

"I see." He leans in and kisses Molly on her cheek. "I was just worried about you. Yesterday was an awful lot to take in."

"Well, I'm doing fine," leaning to her side, the cramps reminding her, hey, this isn't a good time for you. "My mind has been occupied. You know that lady I interviewed?" Molly asked, backing up and letting Billy in. Before he could nod, "she died. Probably not long after I left. Imagine that."

"Weird, I guess lately your whole life has been a matter of small coincidences."

"Small tragic coincidences." Molly goes to the kitchen and pours two cokes and speaks louder so Billy can hear her. "This is what is strange to me. If whatever sudden affliction, heart attack or whatever, I guess they are not sure, but if whatever happened to her would have happened earlier while I was there, than I could have helped her.”

“Like 911?”

“Stop it, Billy. Don’t joke about that, so many were killed.”

“I’m not meaning to joke or be disrespectful to anyone but think about it.” He reaches out for the coke takes a sip and places it on a coaster before speaking. “All those people and their lives. A few people for whatever reason missed their flight, and as a result they lived. In the wreckage they uncovered date planners, wallets, phones, remnants of a life lived, and now a life lost. Now their last phone calls, their last

appointments that would normally seem casual will be burned into the minds of their loved ones forever.”

“I’m only kind of following you.”

“A person who left to go to work that day never knew it was their last day to kiss their spouse, pet their dog or whatever. A person who called in, missed a flight never knew that they would never see their co-workers again. Yet, they must wonder, gee, why was I saved?”

“A little too deep for me. Besides, that is a little too fresh for me to consider.”

“Is it, I mean, I will never forget the last time I saw Charlie. Leaving, telling mom he loved her, he will be home soon and then in my mind, when I saw him walk out that back door it is almost like in my imagination he is walking into a white cloud. At least that is how I imagine it. And here I am," Billy looks around, sitting in the very living room where he probably took his last breath. I guess I will never know for sure."

"You know," Molly said gently, "Dennison killed a lot of people in different places. It is possible that Charlie didn't die here."

"And it's possible that he did."

Molly thinks of her nightmares, then with a little hesitation she says, "I can get dressed and we can go somewhere. I understand if you don't want to be here."

"Actually, I think we should bless this place."

"Even though Sharon said I should do it alone."

"Oh, I'm gonna let you take the lead, but I am going…" As Billy spoke a man's laughter sounded from the room. "What was that? Is someone here?" Billy said inquisitively and a bit startled.

Molly nervously smiled, "you heard that. I thought I was going crazy." She sets down coke, and then says, "Something is in this house."

"So, the place is haunted?"

"I know that I sound completely crazy, and I know what I said before but, Sharon is right. There is something here and it is trying to torture me. I think it is Dennison. The dreams that I told you about have gotten worse. Last night was horrible." Molly's voice is raising as she speaks talking faster, trying to get it all out. The dreams and even some of the visions are now happening while I am awake. I just don't know what to make of it…" the laughter sounds again.

"Get the fuck out," Billy shouts out. He looks at Molly and holds up his hand, "I believe you." Noticing the bag of items that they had gotten the night before. "Let's do this thing shall we."

Molly gets up, "you get the things out. I've got to go to the little girl's room." She rushes to the bathroom; Billy begins laying out the items when he turns to look at a dark shadow hovering near him. His eyes widen as he sees it form into a man.

"Charlie was it. Ahh, I remember him, so sweet and delicious." The thing cackled at him. "You know I think he enjoyed taking it up the ass." Laughing harder, "what do you think Billy boy. What brings you here. You want to take the same sucking as your brother. Oh, I didn't kill him right away like you hoped. Like you prayed. I kept him around for a few days. I always kept the ones I like for a few days. Enjoying them, screwing them with every imaginable object you can think of. And I did like Charlie." As the thing leered at him, coming closer, Billy body froze in fear, his throat dry and a sticky paste formed in his mouth. "Charlie, Charlie, Charlie, you cried for him all these years. You think he loved you. The pathetic younger brother. He would have loved to get away from you and your clingy mother. You were nothing to more to him than bug needing to get caught in a web. Here you are, grieving him for all these years when he didn't even care about you."

"Shut up, shut up, shut up!" Billy force himself to mutter and close his eyes

"Wish him away, wish him away," another gentle voice said. "If you pray hard enough, you can make him go away. For a moment at least."

22

The Pied Piper's Prince

I think I broke through finally. She heard me. I know she heard me. She knows I am here. I don't know what she is going to do about it, but if she does something than I can be free. Then everyone else can be free. Something bad will happen to Cory. I think he will miss me, but I have seen him be so cruel to so many people, that it will serve him right.

I watch her sometimes. I don't think she knows that I am there when I watch her. She walks around the house at night before she goes to bed with this white smoke coming from this stuff she burns in a small bowl. She uses a leaf to wave the stuff through every room of the house. Almost like the ritual they have on Palm Sundays at church. Only, it's not Palm Sunday. Least I don't think so. I lose track of time so easily. I don't know what day it is much less what time it is. That is sad. Mom would be upset if she knew that I wasn't celebrating Palm Sunday. Ralph would understand cuz he doesn't like to go to church and stuff, but Mom will be mad.

This lady is always speaking out, saying whatever is here needs to leave. Let her have peace. I don't think she really wants me to go, but she does want the others to leave. Or at least Cory, Cory taunts her awfully bad. Don't know why, she never does anything wrong. She's nice. She just sits in front of some screen and types all day long. I think she is afraid that Cory is gonna hurt her like he does everybody else, but he really doesn't want anything to do with women. I think he just wants to scare her off but if he can't do that than he will kill her. I've seen him put enough pressure on her while she is sleeping to have her awake clutching at her throat in fear. He never pushes down on her hard enough to do any real damage, so maybe he just wants her to be scared. Or at least to be able to tell people that he is here.

One night when I was watching her, hoping to creep into her thoughts, I saw him hover over her. He put one hand on her chest and the other he wrapped around her throat. Squeezing. I saw his eyes flare up, a vein in his neck pops out and the muscles in his arm firm. But we are in a different realm than her. His strength is not always strong enough to extend beyond the vale and he knows it. He saw me looking too. I would have thought he would have loosened his grip knowing that I was his prince, but he just said, "say goodbye to your friend. You don't think that I don't know you are trying to conspire with her." I hate it when he uses big words. He knows that I don't always understand. That is when he calls me stupid and a waste and says that he did the world a favor by keeping me, but I still begged him to leave her alone. To let loose of her. She couldn't do anything anyway.

I'm starting to believe that too. "I'm beginning to think that I am beyond the place where I can get help. I'm beginning to think that I will never be a hero."

23

2001

"Lord, I ask you to surround this house with your heavenly light. Cast away the demons that dwell within."

The entity twists his head, in Molly's direction as she enters the room, "May your holy angels fly down to this residence and banish those that do not wish to leave."

"You are stupid, stupid wretched woman. You think you can make me leave with a little dust, smoke, and water. You say your prayers every night in hopes that I won't haunt your dreams. But you forget my dear, you are on my land. This is my house. This is my home, and I will do within the walls that I please."

"I think not," Billy manages to stammer. "You leave here. You are not welcome. This is no longer your home." He holds his camera firmly to his chest.

The entity snaps his head back. "Oh, you are still here. My little altar boy, crying for his brother. Shame you didn't come with him. A twofer. I had plenty of those you know. I could have saved you for last so you can watch him wither away in misery.”

“May your holy angels fly down to bring peace in the name of Christ.” Molly’s posture straightened. Her voice strong. She looks at the thing that has grown into a large dark cloud plastered throughout the room. “I know what you have done in life, but you have no power here. The only place that you are welcomed is hell.” She impulsively threw a bowl of water onto the black mass. It sizzled and dissipated right as Billy managed to take a picture of it.”

A stank filled the air, but the room became silent. Billy was the first to speak in a soft, shaky voice. “Do you think it is gone?”

“No, I think that disgusting thing is only beginning which is why we need to work fast.” Molly had to sit; her cramps were burning through her.

“You look pale.”

“No worries.” She takes his hand as he comes closer. “Just female stuff. Nothing demonic even though it may feel like that. Do you really think that it will show up on a picture?”

“Well, it’s worth a try. Bring some validity to what we are doing? I’ll send it to the Warren’s myself and get some real advice. Do you think that was a demon?”

“No,” Molly speaks slowly, “at least not that. I think that there is evil in this house but,” she hesitates, “I believe that evil resides in humans or, at least in the likes of someone such as Dennison."

"Well, yeah, I just witnessed it."

"For sure, but I do believe that was Dennison in the spiritual form. But I also believe that he is influenced by something far darker. I think it was here when he was alive."

"Yeah, but he was killing kids long before he moved here."

"I know," as Molly spoke, one of the candles she lit sparked up into the air and then flickered out. They both look at it, "I believe he had something horrible attached to him, and it is nestled in here until it finds another place to go." She then looks up at Billy, straight into his eyes, "what if it follows me when I move." Looking around her, "I have said it before, and I will say it again. They should have torn this place down when they discovered the bodies."

24

Within the Vale

"Can they hear us?" Molly asked David quietly.

"Nah, this already happened. I don't figure they can hear us. They can't even hear their own conscience."

Molly looked at the two boys fishing. "Why are they here?"

"They got two more in the van. Sometimes they like to fish before they bury the bodies. This is Cory's place; I think he inherited from his dad too. Like the house. He's got about five or six buried out here. They," David nods to the boys, "they like to take their time. Maybe they have to build up the stomach to do their job."

"Why do you think they do it?"

"Do what?"

"His bidding. You know, bury his dead. It doesn't make sense."

"Can't make no sense out of the mind of psychopaths."

"Do you think they are psycho?"

"They're something. Willie, he likes it." David looks over to Molly, "you know, he could have been the one buried here but instead Cory saved him. Not sure what it was about him. But he liked him and decided that he would get him to get boys to him. Cory picked me up and a few others, but Willie and Boozer picked up most of the boys."

"Dennison picked you up?"

"Yeah. I was looking for Jeremy when he drove up and talked me into getting into the car. I was happy until I got to his house. Once I was there and I couldn't find Jeremy, I wanted to leave. I am not sure when I got scared, but it wasn't long after that I realized that I was in trouble. I mean, I thought I saw Jeremy out of the corner of my eye, like some transparent shadow, but I guess my head was playing tricks on me. Willie though, he was there, and he was real and meaner than a hornet."

"What did they do to you?"

"I don't remember exactly." David twisted his head and looked up. "Course I don't even know how we ended up here. It's like I'm skipping through time."

"Do you know your story?"

"What do you mean?"

"What Dennison did to you? How you died?"

"What are you talking about?"

25

2001

Molly got out of bed. Her legs were shaky. She looked down, noticed the blood trickle down her leg. Great. Is this going to be a daily occurrence? Why am I bleeding so hard? She thought as she pulled herself up and stumbled to the bathroom. The days and nights were so mashed together, she barely got sleep and she was always on edge. There have been times she thought she should have taken Billy up on his offer for her to come and stay with him. It would be so much easier to just walk away. Let some other innocent people move in and take on this burden. Her conversation with Billy burns in her mind.

"We just aren't there in our relationship," she tells him through his gentle arguing that he had a spare room. The truth was, she hated living with people, yet now with the constant visions in daylights as well as her dreams, the occasion rattling of an appliance, the flickering of a light, the disembodied voices and cackles that whispered in the air, it felt like she was living with a paranormal circus. Sometimes she felt scared, sometimes she felt great sadness and other times her anger raged through her, and she wanted to punch the walls.

Molly knows that David is harmless. Not just with Sharon's reassurance but his own childlike innocence is astonishing. He has no clue he is dead, nor can he tell the past from the present. In her dreams he takes her on these journeys which aid in providing enough detail that she can now do some authentic research into the horrendous events that happened in this house during the seventies. It is now time take the rein in her hands and discover details that are not listed in any old papers. But not here, researching at home was not going to work. Dennison, dead as he is, always seems to be one step ahead by tapping into her thoughts, which is the last thing she needed. "Paranormal interference. A real thing" she says out loud to the house. When she goes to the paper, Eddie hounds her for trivial stuff eliminating that option, leaving her to the mercy of the outdated public library. The internet access is but the micro phish film collection along with archived old newspapers is extensive. Too bad the librarian would not allow coffee near the computers. A true disgrace to the research process. That and smoking menthols, dropping ashes on crumpled papers pretending to be sixties cool.

Molly scours masses amount of news articles, blurry video reels and clippings regarding all the lost and missing boys. Some of the news footages tried to link missing people all the way from Canada. The horrors of the Dennison's crimes were to no avail. Confirmation of his rapes and tortures, the devices he used to enhance his experiences made Molly's stomach twist and ache even more than it already did. And yet, she trudged on to learn every disgusting piece of information about that sick thing is in her house. Watching her, invading her dreams, crushing her and that David. David, poor David. Trapped in a looping nightmare for eternity. She could leave but he feels trapped, obligated and hopeless.

When she came across the articles that showed Dennison's nude body lying dead in the hallway, her thoughts deepened. He died there. He lived and died there as well as many of the young boys that he killed. How was his life celebrated, and where was he laid to rest? This must be what Billy had talked about when he was examining her hallway.

Digging further she discovers that Dennison's grave is in a cemetery that is less than ten miles away. A marked grave at that. God how disgusting, she thought. People celebrating the life of their loved ones and within a few feet lies the resting place of a serial killer. Someone like that doesn't deserve to be placed in an area where others walk so freely to visit their dearly departed. Molly thought while gritting her teeth. How does something like that happen? Tears water the grounds around him, an he, his rotting corpse has certainly liquified into the roots of the tree just past his stone pillow.

"Ma'am," a polite voice interrupts her thoughts, "I'm sorry, but we close at four today. You are welcome to come back tomorrow."

Molly looked up at smiled at the old lady librarian looking down at her. She was probably very pretty at one time, Molly thought. Her eyes were ice blue and her teeth if they were still hers seemed perfect. "I'm sorry, I've been doing some research."

"The lady looked down at her computer. "On Cory Dennison I see. What interest do you have on that pathetic disgrace?"

Molly felt uncomfortable. How do I tell this lady that I am living in his house where he killed many people and I have reason to believe that he is haunting me with along with one of his victims only he doesn't know he was a victim nor does he know that is he dead, and lets also talk about the demon that is hanging around. Instead, Molly smiled, "morbid curiosity. I'm a writer, and well, I'm thinking of possibly doing a story."

"Well, I would think that was storied out. Unless of course they found another body."

"Wait, they didn't find all the victims?"

"They don't think so. I heard that the Harris County lab is still running DNA on old mismatched bones they have in their storage from that time."

"I read that they were trying to link him to many different missing men, but it doesn't make sense. I mean, most of the pictures of the men didn't fit his MO. Plus the Gacy murders happened near the same time."

Her eyes were saddened as she bent down to pick up some books next to an empty computer seat. "Well, I don't believe that all the boys were reported, or the police were so certain that they were runaways that they did not even bother to investigate if there was a connection."

"Did you live around here when this all happened."

The lady sighed. "It was all so sad. I was small so I don't remember much but my sister Hillary, she knew some of the boys." She sets her books down and sits beside Molly and holds her right index finger to the desk upright. "You see, the house on Winkle Street was here, and we lived on the street behind it." She uses her left index finger to indicate her home, "I was small, not even in school yet. My mom had just dropped off Hillary and she was driving us back and there they were. A trail of police cars of different kinds." Sitting straight up, "we never had a scene like that happen here. This was horror movie stuff. We didn't know what happened. I was staring out the window, but my mother said to stop gawking, but I just couldn't take my eyes away from it. It was nobody's business what was happening at that house." Her voice drifted and her eyes hazed over, "she was like that, mind your own biscuits she'd say, that way nobody would come a questioning about yours." Taking up the books again, "I wish to God, that people didn't mind their own biscuits. Maybe those boys would be alive. When something happens right under your nose, well then, I believe it is your biscuits." Standing up, "that sick bastard raped them you know." Straitening her skirt "right there in the heart of an American suburb, the most grotesque of crimes occurred." Looking at Molly, "I caught a glimpse of that kid that shot him. Wild haired boy, being pushed into the police car. Will never forget that look. Best I could describe it was the look that Charles Manson had when he was being led out of court."

Molly swallowed hard, thinking about the visions that she has spent the last several nights being haunted by. "I know. He tortured them. I saw the boards he handcuffed them too."

"I can't believe they would put such gory stuff on the news."

"Sure," Molly said with a weak smile. "Can you…" she hesitated for a moment, considered, and decided to ask her question anyway. "Can you tell me about him? Cory Dennison that is? Did you ever have any interaction with him?"

"No, can't say that I have. Daddy use to hire Boozer, his friend, you know, one of the boys that he used to help lure the others to him. You know, the one that claimed he never took part in any of the killings," as she spoke, she used her fingers to create air quotes with the books still close to her chest. He seemed nice enough. Anyway, he'd come and mow and rake the lawn. He did it several times and when he was done, he'd come in, mother would give him a cold drink, a coke or something and he'd chat with the family, just like any normal teen. Nobody never thought much of him. Just a friendly kid. A little odd, but friendly."

Molly shuddered, "What do you mean, a little odd?"

"Standoffish I guess, when asked about family and school. I guess he may have dropped out by that time, but still, he didn't raise any red flags regarding being dangerous or anything like that."

"That just makes the whole tragedy even more scary." Molly said with a sigh.

"Well, I guess, you never really know people."

"You seem to think he took part in the killings?"

"Who Boozer, why I guess I just assumed he did. I figured he was lying. I mean, it wasn't like he was being held hostage at the house. Sure, he stayed with Cory for a while on and off again. But you know that kid, he could have told someone what was going on and he never did it. He could have told his dad."

"Well from what I read, his dad wasn't any good anyway or at least didn't seem to care for him."

"That may be true but, he could have gone to someone. The world is filled with someones, it is just a matter of finding the right someone to listen."

"From what I have read, he didn't have anyone but Dennison. I figured that he was so desperate for love of any kind that he would have done anything to please him."

"Well, if you ask me, he was sick. I mean, Boozer knew what Dennison was up too. And even if he didn't kill anyone, he sure as hell helped bury those bodies. One call. One call to the police, or a visit with a neighbor, something, could have helped save those boys life and he did nothing. Had to be a little sick in the head if you ask me," shaking her head, "there is always a someone."

"Didn't the other one tell his mother and she didn't believe him or something."

"Oh, horseshit on that. What mother is going to let their kid hang out with a man after being told the horrific stuff that he was doing. Even if she didn't believe her son, she should have been disturbed by the accusations. But no, she let him continue to go on over there. If anything, she should wander where he was getting all his cash that he threw around here and there. He liked doing what he was doing. Got off on it even. Hell, I think he may have been just as bad as Dennison, if not worse."

"How do you mean?"

"Well, the way that I figure, Dennison did not have any real true connection with any of those missing boys. At least not after the candy shop closed. That is why he needed the other two to help him. That Higginbotham kid, well, he brought in people that believed that he was their friend. He literally led them to their death. He admitted as much. From what I understand, shot them right smack in the head. It's sick. Can you imagine holding a gun on a friend, looking at them straight in the eyes as they are pleading for their life and shooting them execution style. Those boys, the last thing that they thought of was not necessarily that I have been violated in the most personal way possible, or the blood that was oozing out of their orifices, but how their friend betrayed them. Let it all happen to them." She shuddered, looked down, "I can't even begin to imagine what was going on through their minds. Sick, I tell you, sick."

Molly let the words of the librarian sink in. The lady started to push in chairs and with a slight hesitation, she turns back to her, "my sister Hillary, her boyfriend disappeared. They were only thirteen at the time. He left school one day and then was not seen alive again. It would be a year before his body would be dug up at a storage shed, not too far from here." She begins to walk away, "a person never forgets a thing like that. No matter how old you get. It is a stain in my memory to the day I take my last breath."

26

The Pied Piper's Prince

The house is quiet now. I like it when it is quiet. It is not always quiet. Even when it is empty. Course I like it when people come to stay awhile. But when they leave, and they always leave, people come to clean it out and dig up the back yard. Convinced they are going to find some magical treasure or something. They did find bones once and they seemed excited about it. Cory only laughed as he watched the spectacle. Said it was those of a dog. He laughs a lot when people come in and out. Running through all their family traditions in a home. This one couple even did a mock funeral service. Set a coffin right in front of the front window, you know like they did in the old history books. I thought it was a Frankenstein funeral and that made me laugh but Cory said it was a frankincense burning cuz they wanted us leave but he said we ain't going nowhere and none of their Voodoo witchcraft was gonna make him go.

I hate it when they burn white sage around the house. I thought about telling Molly that because she does it a lot. I mean, she is practically doing it every day. Ralph would say she was obsessed or something and Mom would say she's crazy. Cory just laughs when she does it and calls her a stupid ho. She seems to think that this house is evil, but it is not the house. All the house is, is a combination of bricks and wood with some cement. I even overheard her friend Billy tell her that once. He is so nice; she should listen to him. She needs to know that Cory is the one that is messed up in the head. If he would just leave people alone then everyone would stop bringing in the mojo healers and stuff. Sometimes the people will holler out that they want to lead us into a better place, but Cory says that there is no better place than a man's home and he ain't leaving. He then snickers that the only leading will be done is him taking them straight to hell.

27

2001

Molly entered through her front door. The librarian's words still on her mind. She looked around the undisturbed house was undisturbed embellished by her messy desk, crumbled candy wrappers, and an empty coke can that had been sitting on the coffee table for three days. She slipped off her shoes, drops her bag on the kitchen counter and pads into the bathroom.

Damn it, bled through again. Molly was used to having long cycles, but this one seemed to be lasting extra-long, giving her massive cramps and clots. God, I hope this isn't endometriosis again. Her phone rings, she had left it in the kitchen. Quickly throwing off her pants, she wets a washrag and puts it between her legs and runs through the house in the direction of her phone tripping right before she reached it.

"Shit," she cried out in agony. She fell on her left knee, the one already eaten up with arthritis and watch it instantly turn blue. She reaches up for the phone. Billy's number flashed and then voicemail notification. He wants to go out, she thought, cursing herself for not having the same network as him. A text message would be convenient now, she thought, not wanting to call him back but knowing she needed to.

She pulls herself up and limps to the bathroom, checks the washrag, already covered with congealed droplets of blood. As she begins to clean herself, a disembodied voice snickers out, "Ah, I bet Billy Boy would love to taste that."

A shiver of icy fear beginning at the base of her neck shoots down her spine. Her heart jumps, her mouth goes dry, her stomach twists as she drops to the toilet seat, a tear coming out of her left eye. Slowly and steadily, she gets up, cleans herself up and puts on some pajama bottoms. She pulls out a candle that the cashier at the psychic bookstore had carefully wrapped in tissue paper and unwraps it with much less fragility. She lights it and walks around the bedroom. In a steady, loud, firm voice she begins commanding, "Lord in Heaven, I beg of you to send down your angels to battle alongside me to protect me from the assaults of the evil that resonates within these walls."

A cackle of laughter flickers the candle. The lights bounce on and off, "you stupid, stupid woman. You think God hears you. You fat cow. You are nothing more than a speck of dust on the earth. You mean nothing to no one. You write your fantasy romance novels so that horny housewives can masturbate to them, but I got news for you. Even they are bored with your words. You are not even worth the phlegm of the most diseased specimens that rot the earth."

Molly shakes her head, "Please forgive the sins that have been committed in this room by the hand of the dwellers before me." An ominous wind picks up in the bedroom, her bedside lamp tips over, a book is flung at her by invisible hands. "Grant those sinners the ability to see the wrongs of their ways, to seek your grace and forgiveness."

The taunting voice hovers over her, "you won't let Billy Boy touch you will you. Afraid he will be disgusted by your fat folds and bulging thighs."

"Dispel the powers of darkness that hides from your light…"

"Your God will not answer, he does not hear you as he does not care,"

"Protect me this night as well as any others who finds themselves lost, in this room."

"May hell's angels devour you!"

"Jesus, I put my trust in you. I beg of you to save me."

"The life is draining out of you woman,"

Molly's phone rings, she grabs it. Her candle light blows out and she muffles, help me and falls to the ground unconscious.

28

Within the Vale

"You make it so easy. I should just kill you now!"

"Leave her alone! Please!" David begs.

"Shut up Prince. This is your fault. If it wasn't for you, she wouldn't have known we were even here."

"Then blame me. Punish me."

"Nah! You are no use to me now. You have never been any use. Just something pretty to look at." Dennison walks over towards David. "I've been done with you years ago."

"Then let me go. Let me go home to Mom and Ralph. Please!"

"You stupid moron. You really think you could just go home. You really think your mommy and your bubby wants your stupid ass. Stupid boy. You have been forgotten years ago."

Molly laid motionless on the floor. Physically paralyzed, mentally frantic. Hearing the voices, seeing gray shadows between flickering eyelashes."

"She's in here," a strong voice breaks the vale.

"Just let go you wretch of a woman."

"Leave her alone!"

"Her vitals are weak; it looks like she lost a lot of blood." How is he breaking through? Molly thinks but unable to respond. Then she hears Billy's scared voice.

Billy wipes sweat off his forehead, "will she be, okay?"

"We got to take her in."

"What hospital."

"Southeast. They have a better triage unit than Bayshore." The other paramedic looks up at Billy and with a compassionate voice, "don't worry, they will take good care of her." The voices become muffled as they all blur together.

"Die bitch!"

"Leave her alone."

"Hey, isn't this the house…"

"Scott!" the female paramedic lets out harshly. He looks back at her, catches her sharp glare, "okay, let's go. I'm calling it in."

Billy picks up the bloody towels left behind. "He finds a bag in Molly's closet and rummages through her drawers picking out clean cotton panties and pajamas, completely oblivious to the cackling and taunting, inviting Billy to stay.

"Let's have a party, Billy Boy."

Billy takes the dirty clothes and puts them on top of the washing machine hesitates and then pulls down the Tide from an open shelf and starts a load.

"I got something for you to play with."

Billy checks his phone, grabs his keys and notices Molly's on the counter and grabs them. Then, taking one last look around the house, he feels what seems like a hot breath released on the back of his neck. Forcing himself to not look back, he grabs Molly's purse and charger, shuts off the lights and closes the door.

"Leaving so soon Billy Boy? But why? Your brother wants company."

29

The Pied Piper's Prince

"I don't know why he does the things he does. Sometimes I wonder if he even understands. His thoughts led by the devil. His sick games, chanting at others. Saying evil nasty words. He laughs when I try to leave. He says that I belong to him and that there is no way out. I don't like to say anything back. I used to pretend like I didn't know what he meant when he would tell me I was too pathetic to get out. He cackles out a loud snapping noise when I zoom around the room trying to tug doors and windows but not even able to grasp onto a latch or doorknob. My ideas of escaping are constant. He knows it too and his comments bother me, but I don't let it show. I usually just go to the bedroom and crouch down in the corner and watch the other shadows go by.

Sometimes he goes into the middle of the hallway, he puts his head against the wall and stares down. Don't know what he's looking at and I don't know why but he'll will just stand there. No emotions, no sobs, just quiet like and then he will start back up again. I don't say anything. The less that I talk to him, the easier it is for him not to be reminded that he has me trapped. That I am his property and there is nothing that I can do about it.

Molly doesn't belong to him though. I can't even imagine why he would bother to try and keep her here. She serves no purpose to him. In fact, all she does is aggravate him. I should just tell her to leave. Get out before he figures out a way to make her stay.

30

2001

Molly opens her eyes. A pretty nurse with olive complected skin and a round face looks down at her. She smiles, "well hello, welcome back."

Molly tries to sit up but realizes she can't get a grip of the bed. "What happened?"

"Well, according to your chart, you were hemorrhaging something awful." She wraps a cuff around Molly's arm, "but you are on the mend now. I think you will be just fine. Your blood pressure is good," she speaks as she is writing down numbers and checking her watch. "I'm going to let the doctor know that you are awake. Are you hungry, you missed dinner?"

As Molly was about to answer she heard a knock on the door. It is Billy standing with a modest but beautiful flower arrangement. White daisies and yellow roses gathered in a snail vase. "Well, hello beautiful."

Molly blushed, not sure if it was because she knew that was a lie or because she could not remember the last time anyone had bought her flowers. The nurse pats her hand, "My name is Grace, and I am going to be your nurse this evening. Now you visit with your friend. I am going to go check to see if I can scrounge up a snack for you. Do you have any questions before I leave?"

"Is Big Brother on tonight?"

"Oh my gosh," Grace squealed, "I love that show. Yes, it is, I will be back before it starts and make sure we can find it for you." Molly smiled as the nurse exited out of the room.

Billy pulled up a chair and his voice softened."

"Molly, what happened?"

"I have awfully bad periods. Hope you aren't looking for a serious relationship where you can have kids, cuz there's a good chance you won't get that from me."

"Molly, do you think something else caused this?"

Molly thought of the last visions and voices she heard before she fell unconscious. She started to tell him, but she felt tired and foolish, so she simply answered, "what do you mean?"

"I don't know. It's just when I was cleaning up in there, I felt like something was watching me and with what we heard the other day and…"

"Billy, it is strange being in someone else's home when you are not there. Especially mine. After all the stories that I told you and what you…" she hesitates, "what we both heard when we made a feeble attempt to bless the place, well, regardless, even on a good quiet day, it is easy to let imaginations make the better of you.”

“Well, you may think I’m weird or hell, even a nutcase but, those negative energies that we have both been subjected too are more powerful than either one of us. Even with all of our discussions, I would never have thought that something that is not in our physical realm could attack a person but maybe this is no coincidence. For the most part, I thought that this was just the environment and the gossip attached to it and hell, even the mind can create disturbances to scare the crap out of someone, but I am thinking different now. I think you are being attacked. Those pictures that I took during our blessing attempt came out with black splotches in different areas of the house. Including the hallway.”

“I know I heard and saw things before this happened, but I also know that my uterus has been my physical nightmare since I was thirteen. As much as I would like too, I can’t blame everything on ghosts.”

“I wouldn’t be so sure. I am convinced that something unseen is getting to you. Whatever it is, I did catch it on film. You know, there are some convincing stories about how people believed that negative spirits have attacked their psyche or something, pulling on their emotions, causing havoc in the family unit. Perhaps they can attack the physical person. You know, in those ghost shows on the travel channel, you hear about how they attack animals and many of the pets die.”

"I'm not a house cat," Molly said with an uneasy chuckle.

"Think about it Molly. Dennison died right there in that hallway of your house. Right where the black smudge appears on one of the pictures. Not far from where you collapsed."

"I was in my bedroom."

"The same room where all those murders took place. Maybe Dennison himself is the one screwing with you. Your thought process and your emotions." Lowering his voice, "maybe he is trying to torture you."

"So, you think Dennison's spirit is now attacking me?"

"Yes," Billy said softly.

"Look, I have a lot of anxiety. Eddie is giving me crappy stories, which I have to take because I need the money, my books aren't selling unless I turn them into some sort of erotica and every time it is that month of the worse, it gets worse and lasts longer. As you can see."

"I saw the candles when I was cleaning up. Something happened right before I called, didn't it?"

More like during it, Molly thought, but she let out a smile. "Billy, I am so tired. Thank you for everything but I need to get some rest."

"So, you can watch Big Brother," Billy said in a more positive tone.

"Yeah, so I can watch Big Brother."

"Do you need me to do anything for you."

"Can you evict a demonic spirit?" Billy sighs but Molly lets out a smoothing smile, "just check on the house. Make sure it is locked up. Don't need some stupid kids lurking around getting any stupid ideas."

"Will do. And I will be back tomorrow as well." He bends down and kisses her forehead as Grace came in carrying a sandwich and two juices. "I'm going to go to your house right now and make sure everything is safe and secure."

Molly started to ask if he felt safe going there alone but with Grace in the room, she decided against it. Be safe, be safe, Molly thought to herself.

Billy headed out, passing a busy nurse's station and several open doors, visitors saying their hellos and goodbyes as if being in the hospital was an invitation for a family reunion. Well, the only time my extended family gets together is for weddings and funerals he thought."

Dusk was settling over the parking lot. Billy looked up at the bluish orange illuminating the sky. He takes a deep breath and starts up his car. "And in local news," the radio announces out, "Harriet Stokes, beloved librarian of the Pasadena City Library has passed away yesterday in her sleep."

Billy turns the dial and finds the oldies country station and turns up Cross my Heart by George Straight. The drive to

Molly's was a short one, but not short enough to prevent a building up of anxiety. I got to do this. Not just for Molly but for Charlie, Billy thinks as he takes a deep breath turning onto Winkle Street. The front porch light glowing, waiting, beckoning. The small narrow steps to the door, smiled like gnarling teethe.

Ground yourself Billy, slow your heart. "Too late Billy Boy, I know you are here," a voice cranked up in his head. He opens the door. The first thing that catches his eye is the lumps of clutter that are around the house. Molly's cute, but she's not a housekeeper, that's for sure. He remembered once, his aunt who was all into mystic stuff telling him that the first thing to do before cleansing a house spiritually was to clean it physically, claiming that if the house is cluttered than the mind would be cluttered too. His dad often said that his aunt was a nutcase but just in case, he began cleaning up the scattered dishes, empty cans and bundles of laundry that didn't make it to the hamper. He threw the load from the washing machine to the dryer and set another one of towels and jeans.

"Wow, you must really like that cow," he hears. It's not real, it's not real, he mutters out loud as he continues to clean without looking up. He walks to the bedroom and finds Molly's stash of candles and sage on the dresser. He lights a candle, "I declare this house a sanctuary of peace and I exile all negative, detrimental and toxic evil energies that fight to reside here."

"Oh, you and your stupid fancy words. You will not make anyone go away."

Billy walks around the house, reciting the chant in each room. "I deny your presence, I will any unwelcome spirit gone in the name of the lord."

"You are unwelcome!"

"Get out!" Billy continues to chant.

The entity bellows, "die!"

Billy winces as a wind blows through the house, the lights flickier and the rotting smell of old meat fills the rooms, nauseating Billy and weaking him with each step.

"Leave from here. Leave Molly alone! Leave Charlie Alone!" Billy yells before falling to the coach, sobbing uncontrollably. Charlie. Charlie. A child's voice echoes in the room, Billy help me!

Billy looks up and is met with a sharp wind slapping his face accompanied by a wicked laugh. Thee front door opens on its own.

"Get out pathetic boy!"

Billy's head began to pound, and the meat smell burned his nose. He closed his eyes tight and then opened them, but his reality submerged into a hallucination of rotting flesh and white maggots crawling through muscles and veins. A stereo comes on, the knobs turn magically on its own and Harley Poe's voice screeches out, 'the worms crawl in, the worms crawl out". Billy pulls himself up, looks at the candle which had already gone out. The radio blaring, "Did you ever think when the hearse goes by," Billy rushes out, the door slams behind him, "you'll be the next to die."

Billy looks behind him. The house went silent. The music turned off. Just a small, wicked whisper sounded in his ear, "Get the fuck out!"

31

Within the Vale

"Why did you bring me here?" Molly asked the young man, whose eyes fixated on the storage shed door.

"Because I wanted you to know. I need you to know."

"Know what?"

"That evil doesn't just start with one person."

"What do you mean?"

"I guess what I am trying to say is that evil begins as a seed and when it is carefully watered and nurtured and cared for, it grows, sometimes into a wild animal or a carefully calculated demon that waits until just the right moment to pounce. You see, the one that plants the seed is cunning. The grooming is indirect, and it is fueled by the pan of society and digested by innocent bystanders not realizing that they have fallen into an ambiguous trap. Meanwhile the planter is embedding their malice and nurturing ideas to create suffering. Think about it." David turns to Molly, his eyes intent, his words more fluid, intellectual even. More than she had heard from him in the past. No stutter, no drifting. He had direction although his message seemed allusive.

"Think about it," he says again. "When people think of human evil, the picture of Hitler comes into mind, yet he was born. A baby, which became a man. Just an ordinary man. He wasn't tall or attractive or anything special. Except perhaps, his gift of magnetism that allowed him to give a persuasive speech which led to him leading a nation. The Third Reich." He pauses for a moment before adding, "he uses his God given gift to create evil." David looks straight ahead again at the storage shed, "when he was a baby, in his mothers' arms, nobody would have thought that tiny child would lead a torturous savagery, that he did. That he would unleash a conflict that would lead to the genocide of an entire population. But he did. People think that they can avoid evil by minding their own business, and that if we spend our energies on church, Easter Egg hunts, and other positive things that humanity disciplines themselves to focus on than the idea of evil will go away. Disappear, simply because they choose not to think about it."

David got quiet, Molly did as well, digesting David's words. Looking up at the stars, feeling the wind, much to real to be a dream, she broke the silence.

"Thank you."

"For what?"

"For stopping Dennison from strangling me."

"You know?"

Molly nods, David continues to speak, "I am not sure if he still has the power to do so. If he does though, he will. He enjoys things like that. He doesn't put any thought into it. He just does it. It's a game for him."

"I'm not sure that I agree on your thoughts of evil, but I do think that some people become desensitize to it. Cory Dennison being one of them."

"I have seen the look in his eyes when he is strangling the life away from someone. He enjoys it. He is not desensitized; he feeds on it."

"Perhaps he had other influences."

"What do you mean?"

"Well, wasn't it one of Hitler's confidants who said that you don't know the devil when his hand is on your shoulder. Maybe, something else was placed into Dennison's life and he didn't even know it. Perhaps, Dennison wasn't even aware he was evil until the end."

"He has been inflicting pain onto others his entire life. He gets joy from it, he invites others to partake in his fantasies, that is evil."

"David," Molly hesitates, then sighs, "David, Dennison's dead."

"What?"

32

2001

Molly opened her eyes; she could hear a new nurse shuffling around in her room. She sounded larger, heavier on her feet, clumsier.

"Where's Grace?"

"Oh, her shift was over at seven. She'll be back tonight. I'm Olivia. How are you feeling."

"Like, I just got ran over by a mac truck."

Olivia smiled, "I can check on your pain meds."

"No, it's not that, just pure exhaustion."

"That is understandable. You have lost a lot of blood, but the doctor seems to have that under control. You should eat some breakfast though; you need to gain your strength." Olivia picks up Molly's chart hanging on at the end of the bed. "No diet restrictions. That's good. They are coming around with the trays now."

"I am hungry." Looking around, "do you know when the doctor will be in?"

Olivia let out a little huff, "the doctors come when the doctors come, I guess they figure that you have nothing better to do than to wait around for them."

"Well, I guess I don't. Do you happen to know if my friend brought my cell phone?"

Olivia looked around, then notices a small flip phone charging by the sink, "Here is one. Since you don't have a roommate yet, I am guessing this is yours."

She reaches out for it. "That's it." Olivia hands it to her and then checks her blood pressure. Molly's eyes scan the room, taking in a small arrangement of flowers on the nightstand and a drawing that looked like a child had completed. "What's all that?"

"Well let's see, the flowers have a card that says Pasadena Citizen wishes you a quick recovery." Looking it up and down and then at her, "you a reporter or something."

Molly smiles, "something. Who is the picture for?"

Olivia clicks her teeth which somehow makes her ponytail flip, "It says from Jeremy."

"I don't know a Jeremy,"

"Well, I didn't deliver it. It was probably meant for another patient." As Olivia spoke, an orderly brings in a tray of food.

"Bout time you got here, trying to starve our patients I see." The orderly gave her a flirtatious grin. Olivia looks back at Molly, "don't you worry now, Earl here will take good care of you. Slip in a few treats if he likes you enough."

"Well, I'll take what I can get, I am famished." A young doctor with dark complected skin, kind eyes and curly black hair that came just under his chin walks into the room, carrying an air of confidence."

"How's the patient," his voice gentle, his gaze fixated on her, "it has been quite a night for you." As he spoke, Earl offered Molly a salute, put his hands together in prayer form, bows, and then exits the room. Olivia helped Molly sit up straighter and brought her food tray closer.

"What happened?"

"You hemorrhaged out a good amount of blood, losing a fifth which is the most I've seen in a while I might add. We had to give you several infusions, but it seems like we have it under control, however we can't keep exchanging out the blood you are losing." For the first time, Molly notices the IV lines encircling her arm and splintered into her a bulging vein feeding her blood.

"Geez, I had no idea what was happening. Thought it was just a bad period. I've always had them."

"Well, how would you like to not have them anymore?"

Molly got silent, "I guess you are talking hysterectomy." Feeling briefly saddened, "I wouldn't be able to have children then?"

"No, not physically, but there are many options for you to have kids. For the sake of your health however, I must urge you to consider having a hysterectomy. Now we can still leave your eggs if you want, or I can send in some specialists who can go over different options for freezing them…"

As the doctor spoke, Molly's brain began to get foggy. These were words she did not want to hear. Not that her biological clock was ticking or anything like that. Kids was never even on her radar since she has yet been able to find herself in a serious enough relationship that she would want to have a child, but not thinking about it for the present time is a lot different than realizing the possibility will be taken away forever. "Do I need to make a decision now?"

"No, but this will happen again. As you can see, even as early as this morning we had to give you a transfusion." He comes closer, his soft voice lowers even more, "I know this is a difficult idea to process, but I must warn you, if you want a child, you must go ahead and conceive and soon. The next time you may not be as lucky." His voice rang in her head. "Eat your breakfast and I will be back this afternoon."

"Do you need anything else?" Olivia's voice broke her thoughts as Molly digested the doctor's words."

"Uh yeah, I guess not. Hey, I didn't catch that doctor's name."

"It's Doctor Sumadi. Handsome, isn't he?" Molly nodded, as she took a bite of sausage and picked up the phone to call her mother.

33

The Pied Piper's Prince

I don't know what happened to Miss Molly. I don't know what happens to anyone I try to talk to. I'm sure Cory did something to her, but I am not sure what. I never know how to figure out his motives. It's useless. I don't know why he has to be so mean. Mom says that some people were born mean. That they can't help themselves. She said that would explain why small kids do mean things. They don't know why they do mean things unless it is because they enjoy it. I had asked Mom once about prisoners of war and how their capturers might torture them. She said that it was one thing to be a soldier and having to take in a hostage for negotiation purposes, but that a person who takes someone in and then proceeds to torture them is on a whole new level of mean. She would say that there was no rationale for that kind of mean. That when questioned, about why they act that way, they can't give out a reasonable answer because they don't know the answer even though they are the ones doing it. I wonder if it is like that for Cory. I wonder, if he was Hitler, would he order the genocide of all those people in camps as easily as he did the execution of those boys. I wonder if Willie is like those soldiers in the Third Reich who obliged to do Cory's bidding for him. He and Boozer are always so anxious to please him. I wonder if Willie is trapped like me. I mean I see him walk out the door, something that I can't seem to do. He never answers when I call out to him. I see him come back in and often with new friends for Cory to play with. I wonder if he ever thought about walking out of the door and never coming back. Just keep walking. Would Cory go after him?

Is Cory truly evil? Is Willie or Boozer truly evil? It seems that evil would be a disease, not like my dyslexia or my stuttering or my grandpa's cancer. But a disease of the soul. If someone was born that way, like Mom says then that would be an affliction. But Pastor Gary says that most people are good, they just need to be directed on the right path. So, if most people are good, then the idea of someone being born evil would be rare. Thrown out the window like the dishwater as grandma would say. Leading to wonder if the idea of three people coming together with the same affliction is farfetched. Unless Mom is wrong, which would be hard to believe because she is seldom wrong; and what about Pastor Gary. Is he wrong too? Is my gut wrong? Maye evil is contagious. Somehow, Cory inflicted evil onto Willie and Boozer like a nasty cold, but then, who inflicted it onto him? Regardless, if evil can be passed on, then what is the cure, and can it be administered before it is too late. How would someone know if they have been infected or would their brain be so contaminated that they don't care. By the time that they realize that they have caught the disease, it is too late. The damage is done and the infected have lost their soul.

34

2001

"Are you sure you don't want to come home with me? I don't think it is a good idea for you to be alone for the first few days."

"Mom, I appreciate everything, but I am fine. You know how I am; I don't want company when I am not feeling good."

The old woman with her bright red hair and her bright red lipstick huffed, "I am not company, I am your mother. And besides…" Molly's mother looked around the house with a judgmental glare, "why you would want to stay in this place is beyond me. Why anyone would want to stay here, I will never understand. They should have torn this place down years ago."

Molly let out a heavy sigh. "Since when do you have any interest in my home. You wouldn't even have known about it unless I told you."

"Yeah, well I did some asking around at my church. Many of those old ladies were around when this all went down. Do you know how many murders happened here? Over Thirty!"

"That is an exaggeration. I've done my research; he did not kill everyone here and he killed several in other apartments around Houston way before lived he here. You don't see those complexes in the Heights being torn down, do you?"

"Well, maybe they should."

"Well, if everyone had your line of thinking than most of Houston and all of Dallas would be one mass demolished landscape."

"Well, you may be right, but the city of Pasadena should have taken this place down." Molly's mother Lynette walked over to the kitchen, got a glass of water and Molly's prescription but stops short of the hallway. "That's where it happened you know. Dennison gunned down right there."

"In self-defense. Besides, this whole place has had everything restored. New carpet, new counters, and bathrooms. I am living in a modern paradise. Probably the nicest place on this street. Hell, even some of the sheetrock has been replaced." As Molly spoke, her mother walked throughout the house medicine and water still in hand. Molly leans back, closes her eyes and shouts out.

"Can I have my meds please?"

Lynette walks back in, "you know from the occult artifacts I see on your dresser; I am pretty sure you are a bit worried about what resides in this house as well." She walks back in, hands Molly her pills and water and watches her take them before sitting down on the couch opposite of her. The brief silence between them makes Molly anxious.

"What?"

Lynette's eyebrows knits and her eyes squint, "Molly, be honest. Are you comfortable here?"

"I am just fine mother. Really, stop letting the hocus pocus voodoo stuff bother you. Besides, I hardly consider a few candles occult artifacts."

"That is what they are used for, conjuring and stuff. You could be conjuring up Dennison without even knowing it."

"Mother, you are being ridiculous. I have always liked candles and you have never said anything before."

"You like scented ones. The expensive crap from Yankee Candle. These are different. Now I do know you smoke weed against my approval I might add, and although I may not be a sommelier of the product, but tis old' bitty knows the difference between MaryJane and other greens and by my observations that bounded green stuff on your dresser is sage."

"Wow mother, you caught me. I've given up the pot and started smoking sage."

"Don't sass me. I don't care what condition you are in. That is no way to speak to your mother."

Lynette looks around. "I don't like the energy in this place."

"Well ignore it."

"That's just it. You can't. If you ignore it than it can infest you."

"Geez mom, you sound like that voodoo nutcase that Billy took me too."

"See, you do have concerns. Otherwise, you wouldn't be going to see anybody on this. And tell me about Billy. I can't even tell you my surprise when he called me."

"He's just a guy, nothing serious."

"I wish you would talk to me more."

"I try, I just can't handle you jumping to conclusions the way that you do."

"Why, because, I think that the murder house that you live in may harbor a domesticated evil that you are too naïve to understand."

"Exactly! This is a house. Wood and bricks. Just another building that is a part of this world. An object. Objects don't think. They don't lie, they don't breed, and they certainly don't kill."

"Guns kill."

"Not without a finger on the trigger."

"Perhaps Cory Dennison is the trigger."

"That is dead and has been for almost thirty years."

"He almost killed you."

"Oh, my God. You have been talking to Billy. No mother, my messed-up uterus almost killed me. You know, the one that I inherited from your side of the family. The very thing that Aunt Betty suffered from and yet, you never bothered to warn me about."

"Don't go blaming me for your medical mess. Probably too much sex is what caused it."

"Geez mother, you never take accountability. All those times the nurse from school had you come pick me up. The times I passed out due to excessive bleeding and you never thought. Gee, I should probably take my kid to a doctor."

"This again. The lecture of how horrible I am. What a horrible childhood you had."

"Mom, just please go. I need some rest."

Lynette gets up, kisses Molly on the forehead. "Let me help you to bed."

"I'm fine. I think I will sit here and watch some TV for a bit."

"I swear you are the only person that I know that does not have a television in their bedroom."

"It's better in the living room. That way I don't sit up and watch shows when I need to sleep. Besides, I'm more comfortable here. The Lazy boy helps me get up and down." Molly pulls down the handle to demonstrate. I will be just fine."

Lynette looks around and sees Molly's phone sticking out of the pocket of her purse. She goes and gets it and puts it on the charger on the table next to Molly. "You call me if you need anything." Lynette gives her another kiss on the forehead. Molly's eyes are already closing, her consciousness drifting to sleep state not seeing Lynette making the sign of the cross before quietly leaving.

35

Within the Vale

"Wood and bricks you say. You stupid woman." Molly turned her head away from the direction of the disembodied voice, but it only rasped louder penetrating her thoughts. This isn't real, this isn't real. She whispered in her head. This is an illusion. An auditory illusion. "The illusion is not believing what is right in front of you. You think you are too good to have your life infiltrated by the likes of me. A uneducated blue-collar troll. That is your fucked up thinking. You live your too-familiar life in your cozy surroundings with ugly pastel couches and drink red wine and think you are better than everyone else because you published a few trashy books. Molly purses her lips together, too weak to get herself up, she speaks out loud.

"Dear heavenly Father. Protect me from this evil that wishes to…"

A loud raucous laughter vibrates through the house. "Now you are asking God for help. All these years that you have rebelled against him, denied him your worship so you can sleep late and eat cold pizza and make excuses to have your horrid excuse of a mother from dragging you to church and now you seek him." Another release of laughter echoed throughout the house, piercing Molly's ears and she tightens her eye lids while tears squeeze out. "You pathetic cow. You are estranged from God and all of humanity. The only reason why Billy comes around is because he wants to fuck you. He doesn't care about you. He doesn't even care about Charlie. That's right. It is all a ruse to get into your disgusting grandma panties. Are you going to give it to him so he can be disgusted by your bulging lumps of flesh that you squeeze into your girdles hoping to look two sizes smaller? Got news for you cow, one look at your unsightly lymphoedema's and he will be vomiting blood all over this new carpet, wood, and bricks. No amount of mortar will keep me away."

Again, Molly closes her eyes. "Father, I beg of you, stop the obscenities that have entered my life."

Another voice echoes in, "Cory, please stop it. Leave her alone. She's done nothing to you."

Shadows begin to the cloud the room. Another voice hollers out. You've gone too far. We've gone too far. We have to stop."

"Fuck you! I should have killed your ass a long time ago."

Molly opens her eyes and sees the silhouettes of Willie and Dennison in the hallway. Tommy and Tammy still crying on the board. Tammy yells out, "Do something Willie! He's gonna kill all of us."

"You've gone too far Cory. We both have." Willie's hand trembles as he aims the pistol towards Cory. "We've got to stop."

Not this again. Please not this again. I've already seen it too many times. Please God, make it stop.

Dennison leaves Tommy and steps towards Willie, his voice mocking, "you won't do it. You're just a stupid weak little pussy. You won't do it."

Willie fires once, Molly tries to sit up as the bullet barrels into Dennison's chest. He stumbles back but the sure force of adrenaline allows him to get up and lurch forward. With a shocked expression on his face, Willie takes another step towards Dennison and fires two more shots, this time hitting him in the left shoulder. Dennison spins around and exits the room, a thud sounds as he falls into the wall of the hallway. The exact location that Lynette had pointed out a few moments ago. Where Billy stood a week ago.

Willie steps forward. Again firing.

Bang

Bang

Bang

And then silence.

36

2001

Ding Dong

Molly's eyes popped open. She is sweating. She quickly looks down between her legs and lets out a sigh of relief. No blood.

Ding Dong.

The doorbell rings again and Molly recognizes the silhouette of Billy outside the door. She slowly pushes the handle of the lazy boy up and manages to get up and with wobbling feet, walk to the door.

Billy greets her with a smile while holding up a red and white cardboard bucket. "Nothing like the KFC when you got an empty stomach."

Molly lets out a breath. "Thank you. I'm starving."

"I brought some cokes too. Figured with you just getting home, you didn't have time to stock up." Billy walks in and sets the chicken on the table. "Give me a few minutes to get some things out of the car. You can tell me where to find the plates when I come back in. I don't want you to have to do anything."

"You've done enough," Molly said smiling as she slowly walked towards the kitchen. Hollering over her shoulder, "Don't think I don't know it was you that cleaned up…" She stops in her tracks.   "Oh, God!" she gasped. She stares at Dennison's body slumped over in the hallway. Face down, nude, his dark hair stained with congealed blood, his shoulder distorted.

"What's wrong?" Molly turned and looked quickly over at Billy who had his hands filled with eatable treasures, but her hand stretched out toward the hallway.

"It's that," she points and turns back, but nothing is there. Taking a breath. "I'm seeing things again."

Billy stared at her; his eyes crinkled with worry. "I'll be right back."

Molly makes it to the table, she holds her fingers to her temples, The fresh aroma of chicken wafts towards her, without looking up, she pulls the bucket closer to her and pulls out a chuck of breast and eats the skin with the image of Dennison's nude body permeated through her head.

Billy strides in a few minutes later. "Good you're eating. That's a good sign." Molly nods without looking up.

"The plates are in the cabinet over the dishwasher. She listens to Billy rummish through the kitchen, plates clacking together, drawers opening, utensils bouncing off each other. Each sound seeming to have a magnetic effect on her ears. Piercing like a titanites musical. To her it seemed like it took Billy forever to get everything together before he sat down to enjoy the meal with her.

"So how are you feeling?" He asks, sliding a plate of mashed potatoes and beans under her. "We've got gravy too if you want it. I didn't know how you liked your potatoes."

Molly smiled, "this is great. Would've had to order a pizza if you hadn't showed up."

"Yeah, all restaurants should deliver. Grocery stores too for that matter."

"I think some do up north."

"Well, they should down here too."

For a few minutes they ate in silence. Enjoying the food. Molly pulling piece after piece, unembarrassed by the amount of food she was eating. "Guess they didn't feed you well in the hospital."

"Hardly, I'm just happy to be at home." Molly looks around. "Wow, I just realized how creepy that must seem."

"Nah, there's nothing like sleeping in your own bed. Especially when your body has been put through the wringer." Billy looks up from his eating. "That's a fact too. That has nothing to do with the history of this place."

Chewing his food slowly, hesitating before he speaks again. "It just so much bad stuff has happened here. People are unforgiving of places like they are of events. Guess that is why some people do not like to visit their childhood home."

"Yeah, tell me about it. I got into it with my mother earlier." Chewing on her food slowly, "do you think this place is evil?"

"Haven't we had this conversation before."

"Sort of, if just my mother…"

"Oh, yes, Lynette. I had the pleasure of meeting her when we bumped into between visits."

"Funny, she acted all surprised about you."

"Well, maybe she wanted to hear about me before we had the pleasure of sharing your medical emergency together."

"What did you say we were. Our relationship is I mean."

"Well, what is it?"

"God, I hate it when someone answers my question with a question."

Billy covers her hand with his. "I have feelings for you Molly. I was hoping you had feelings for me as well. Especially with me standing by your side with…" Billy's eyes roll towards the ceiling as if someone was up on the fan eavesdropping, "well, you know."

"Billy, did you love your brother?"

Billy sits back and then takes a sip of his coke. "That's an odd question."

"Why?"

"Well, I don't know. I mean he was my brother. I looked up to him."

"Yes, but did you love him. I mean, it is not unusual to have some sibling rivalry. Especially if your parents favored him."

Billy looked at her inquisitively. "What makes you think they favored him."

"Well, I don't know. I mean, I guess I just thought…" Molly bit her lip, trying to remember what that thing told her. Billy kept looking at her. Both enduring the silence harshly before Billy finally decided to break it.

"I'd suppose that brothers have complicated relationships. Much like sisters. I never really felt close to my parents, and they never praised me. Well, not like they praised Charlie. And then when he disappeared," Billy swallows hard, "taken that is; my world changed. Well, to clarify, my home changed, and since home is the world to a child and all things around, friends, teachers, schools, those are just the accessories but home, that was where it was safe. With Charlie being gone, home wasn't safe. It wasn't that I lost this person that I loved so much. He picked on me and bullied me even but, it didn't bother me like it would if it was someone out of my home because he was a part of it. He was my normal and when he was suddenly gone, my normal was taken."

"Well then, you invent a new normal."

"That is just a fancy term that social workers and counselors say to help a person get over a traumatic occurrence that inhabits a person's stability." Billy takes another bite of food and wipes his lips, takes a drink and then says, "there is no new normal. There is just an empty space that goes unfilled."

"I am not sure I follow, or I want to follow."

"You know when you go to the grocery store to buy a common item. Something that you need or use on a regular basis, and you discovered that they are out of that item. Something you count on being there like milk or bread or salt even."

"I don't think I can remember that happening. Not with a common item that is."

"Guess you were safe and tucked away when Allison occurred."

"I remember, that was a bad hurricane."

"Yeah, think about trying to find common items. I went into three stores trying to find milk for my mother. What store runs out of milk for Christ's sake."

"Yeah, well hurricanes bring unusual circumstances."

"And brothers kidnapped and murdered don't?"

"But you didn't know he was murdered yet."

"A part of me knew. I can't explain it, but a small piece of me, a slice of my heart, knew I would never see him again. My mother knew too. She wouldn't admit it, but she knew. She kept the porch light on for years, thinking he will come home. This isn't happening. Her golden child who would never do any harm would come home and beg for forgiveness for being gone so long. But it never happened."

Billy stopped talking, Molly looked at him with comforting eyes. "When did you admit to yourself that you were giving up hope?"

"Hope?" Billy snorts. "Can't say I ever had hope. At least not for Charlie to come home. It was more hoping that mom would be able to handle the news when she finally heard it. That she wouldn't fall into a drunken state, popping whatever kind of pills she managed to get the doctor to prescribe for her so she could numb herself from the realities of the world. I don't think she has ever had the power to confront the hurt and pain of losing Charlie. Her inner demons."

"To confront evil," Molly whispered. "She'd probably became very overprotective of you."

"Hardly, more like I was a burden that she barely knew existed. From that point on, any childrearing I had was placed into the hands of my irresponsible father. Why I drank so young, drove so young, got laid so young for that matter.”

“Have you ever spoken to your mother about the way you feel.”

Billy lets out a laugh, “and let her think that her only living son has feelings. She wouldn’t listen if I tried.” He takes a breath. “But that is all over now. What is important is the present and right now I am happy you are a part of it.”

“Billy,” Molly’s voice had a helpless tone. “I’ve got something to tell you.”

Billy scooches his chair closer to her, “what is it.”

“The doctor said that I need to have a hysterectomy. He said that what happened would happen again and that the best thing to do is to have a hysterectomy. I won’t be able to have children”

“Is that what you are worried about. Sweetheart, if kids are on your mind, there are other ways to get them. As for me, kids are overrated anyway.”

Molly lets out a chuckle. “You mean, you don’t want a little Billy running around just like you?”

“Oh, God no, that kid would be a terror. I figured I could get a dog. A black lab with floppy ears and I would name him Billy. Billy Junior. BJ for short.”

Molly let out a laugh, “you want a BJ?”

Billy laughed too and pulled her closer, "only from you." He leans in to kiss her, the light tapping of rain hits the windows, the room temperature drops three degrees as the lights flicker.

"Billy."

"Yes,"

"My house is evil."

37

The Pied Piper's Prince

I can't believe he did it. Willie. I can't believe he shot Cory. But why is he still here? Torturing everyone that walks through the door. Why? Why is he torturing me? There he is, his body on the floor, and yet standing over it just like he sometimes stands over me. Lingering and snarling. He sounds like a mad animal. Like a hell hound.

One time I attended vacation bible school with a friend. Mom didn't like the church, but I begged to go so she let me. It was fun. Some of the teachers were a little scarier than others. At least in the stories they told. For a while, I was afraid of dogs. Black ones at least. You see, hellhounds are said to be demon dogs that are fierce. They are like the pets of entities and even some angels were said to have them but, I am not too sure about that. The teacher referred to them as soul collectors and they make their appearance to those that are to be, well damn to hell. Sorry for the language but that is what the teacher said. Can you believe it? In church too.

Anyway, once a hellhound decides who they want to attack, supposedly God himself can't help that person. It will never give up until their victim is dead or they are willing to oblige by their master's will and unleash a new kind of evil.

I think that is what happened to Cory. He was attacked by a hellhound. Maybe it didn't rip his body to shreds, but it ripped his soul. I want him to be good. I try to tell him to stop what he is doing. To leave others alone. To help me find Jeremey and we would just go home, get out of his way, and everything would be all right. But Cory wants me to stay, so I agree to stay just to make him happy. I promise to keep being his prince, he just needs to let everyone else go, he gives me that glare. A nasty one where his eyes turn from red to dark and a black smog form around him.

Molly hasn't seen it. I try and protect her from it, but it is hard. Cory roams around, glaring out the window, mocking people who walk by, while Molly lives here, and goes about her life. Cory invisible to her while she is saying her prayers, pacing the floor with her bowl of smoke. When she does that, he circles around her, inventing new ways to create havoc in her life. His favorite technique is to initiate hallucinations. He will kill Molly if he can. No amount of salt or Goofer dust will save her. He will drive her to suicide like he has done to others in the past, or he will find her greatest weakness, mental or physical and drain whatever internal strength she has. And he will stand over her and laugh as she dies, just like he did over his own corpse.

38

Within the Vale

"Why are you just standing there. Get us out of this." Tammy begs Willie who stood over Dennison's corpse in shock.

Molly watches the scene play out in her dream. Her mouth dry, desperately wanting to turn her head towards the cold presence that huddled next to her

"We've got to get them out of here."

"I don't know how to do that," Molly said meekly.

"Why isn't he gone." David whimpered, looking over at Dennison's shadow standing over his own corpse.

Molly watched Willie run over to Tommy and Tammy. First, he unlocks Tammy's handcuffs and then Tommy's who falls to the ground, modestly throwing his hand over his genitals. Crying. A tear drops down Molly's cheek as she notices he is bleeding.

Still with the gun in his hand, Willie paces the house, holding his arms up to his head. "I don't know what to do. I don't know what to do." He turns to Tommy and Tammy. "We won't do anything. We'll just go home and not say anything. Wait until somebody finds him."

"No," Tommy mutters while finding something to cover himself up with. "We have to call the police."

"They're gonna put me in jail. I'm gonna go to jail."

"No, it was self-defense," Tammy pipes in. She runs to a phone hanging on the kitchen wall. It slips between her hands, the yellow cord twisted and tangled together. "We gotta call the police"

"No, don't" Willie picks up the gun and aims it towards her.

Tommy limps slowly over to him, standing a foot taller than he even while using the wall to prop himself up, still not completely dressed. "Willie, what is done is done He would have killed the two of us for sure and probably you too. We got to call the police."

Willie looks over to him, then quickly turns his head towards Tammy and then back to Tommy again. "You're right."

Dropping the gun to his side, Willie walks over to the phone. Tammy had already dialed 911. Willie takes the receiver from Tammy and hollers into the phone.

"Y'all better come here right now! I just killed a man."

39

2001

"Pretty good writing for someone who just had all of their blood drained out of them." Molly smiled at Eddie.

"I never heard you compliment anyone before. At least not me. I'm not sure if you really like the article or you are taking pity on me."

"I take pity on no one."

"Yeah, well maybe you should. It seems death keeps following me around lately."

"What? Ms. Matthews. She had a bad ticker from what I understand. Losing your husband in a freak accident and then having to raise two teens. That will age ya."

"The librarian wasn't that old, and she dropped dead within hours of me talking with me."

"Really," Eddie's eyes knitted, while he focused on her. Thoughtfully, he takes a long drag from his cigarette and leans forward, and in almost a hush voice, "and exactly what were you two talking about."

Molly hesitated, dropped her shoulders and with a sigh, "Cory Dennison."

Eddie leans back, crossing his arms over his belly silent for just a moment before releasing a chirpy voice, "well then go for it."

"What?" Molly asked confused.

"Do a story on the murders. I mean, you live in the house, you have somewhat of a connection to the case," tapping his ashes into a coke can, "maybe even a paranormal one."

Molly swallowed hard and narrowed her eyes, "you don't believe in that sort of stuff do ya?"

"I don't know what I believe, but what I do know is that house has stood empty for many years. You rent it from the bank right. Cuz, they can't sell it, I'm sure. I mean who wants to live in a place like that. Hell, thirty murders were committed in there. That is enough to raise the curiosities of crime enthusiasts."

"Well not that many. When he began his murder spree, he was living in the Heights."

"Ha, so you have already begun your research. So do the story. We'll publish an expose or something. Get folks mind off terrorist attacks."

"I don't exactly want to show tribute to anyone like Dennison's kind. He is a monster."

"Is?"

"You know what I mean. Besides, I don't need any more people snooping around my house with their morbid ideas of seances and stuff."

"It's not your house. It belongs to the bank, and I am sure it will go on the market as soon as your lease is up. Damn place ought to be torn down. I don't care how many makeovers they give that place. New carpet, new counters, new whatever doesn't take away the sins committed in that place. Sick bastard, may he rot in hell for all of eternity."

"Eddie," Molly said slowly, "do you think that if somebody who has passed is afraid of going to hell that might be enough for their soul to linger on."

"Are you trying to tell me that place you are staying at is haunted."

"Do you believe?"

"My wife probably would. Her and her psychics and such. Prefers to get a reading instead of going to a shrink." Eddie stands and goes to pour himself a cup of coffee only to find the pot and lets out a frustrated sigh."

"I think that there is something that may make someone linger. Even if it is a memory." He gets quiet, "when I was sixteen, I was in a bad motorcycle accident, which is how I got this damn scar over my eye and well, we won't talk about how my right leg looks. Anyway, my mother was so worried, and I could hear my dad's voice telling her, trying to comfort her that I was going to be okay. That I would wake up. You know, it was weird, I could hear everything in the room, I even kind of knew what was happening but, I couldn't speak or open my eyes, but I swear, I smelled my grandma's perfume. It was there just as sure as you are sitting there, and this damn coffee pot is empty. I smelled it, and I felt comfort, I felt peace. I talked to my dad once about it a few years later, he just shrugged it off as a way to deal with stress, but I know, I know my grandma was there, visiting me, watching me, lingering until I was out of the woods so to speak."

"Eddie…" Molly paused, took a breath, and began again, this time with more confidence. "Something is in that house."

"Do you want to talk about it?"

"No, I want to write about it."

40

The Pied Piper's Prince

Have you ever thought that you were in a dream even when you were awake? Like the world was not the way you were experiencing it. That is what I am feeling.

When Ralph was born, he came early. He had to be put in an incubator. I didn't know what that was, so I asked my grandmother. She said it was something that will cook him some more so when he comes out of the hospital, he could be healthy. But I didn't know what that meant, cook him some more so I kept asking her to explain it and let me know what it meant that they would keep him in it until they were sure he was completely out of the woods. She said that sometimes doctors give babies treatments because when they are born, they haven't decided if they want to be in our world or not, so they go into the woods. Then the doctors show them how good life is, by giving them a chance to breathe and to know that they are wanted and will be loved.

When I was twelve, one of my mom's boyfriends said he was going to take us on a trip to the Davey Crocket National Forest. I didn't want to go because I knew that forest meant woods and I was afraid death would be there. Waiting for me.

The vines growing around the trees winding around so tight that if you tripped you would fall so hard that there would be no telling what you would smash your head on. If you fell and turned onto your back and looked up, you wouldn't be able to see the sun cuz the tree branches clung together and wrapped around each other like a huddle of arms, shielding the light from coming in. That is why even at three in the afternoon, it feels dark and lonely in the woods. That is where little Red Riding Hood met the wolf, where Hansel and Gretel found the old witches house, where the fighting trees were in the Wizard of Oz, where Willie and Boozer took Mark, Charlie, Matthew and a few others to be buried. A property that Cory has near Lufkin and the Sam Rayburn Reservoir.

Woods are death. I've seen it so many times. Sometimes the same boy, over and over, they cover them with lime powder and roll them up in transparent plastic not thick enough to cover their faces. Leaving their bodies to rot into blobs of putrefied flesh sticking to their bones, the tape plastered over their mouths eroding into tiny strings dropping onto the thin nylon ropes around their necks with sunken in shocked eyes. What they must have thought just moments before the bullet penetrated their skull or the last breath was snatched out of them. Then, with little discussion, Willie and Boozer drive through the McDonald's drive through, with the bodies, slowly turning cold in the back of Cory's van, ordering a Big Mac and Quarter Pounder as if murder and burial made them hungry.

These boys of different ages of the teen years gone. Lost in the woods. I hate the woods.

41

Within the Vale

"David…David…are you here."

Molly had lulled herself to sleep with two leftover Ambien from her hospital stay and stale wine. David stands in the living staring down at bundle in the hallway.

"How did he do it David."

"Do what?"

"Dennison, how did he manage to kidnap so many boys? From the Heights no doubt. That is an upscale area. A busy area, people must have been suspicious. Someone had to see them. Someone had to see that was happening."

David nodded his head and without looking up with a more intellectual tone he responds with, "when a tiger attacks a deer, it is expected. A tiger has to eat, and it attacks what they can conquer. But, when a kitten attacks another kitten, it is not expected. They don't need to eat. They just want to play."

"Are you talking about Boozer and Willie? Are they the kittens?"

David nodded, still looking down. "Is that how Dennison got you? One of them brought you back."

David looked up. "What do you mean?" His voice transformed into the more innocent tone that Molly was used to. "Cory picked me up. He was going to help me find Jeremy. Said Jeremy was with him, cuz he didn't want to go home. I knew that didn't make since cuz Benny and Rose; they are good people. Benny works hard, Rose cooks dinner every night. Jeremy thirteen. He loves his parents. He loves his dog; Bandit and he loves to come and talk to me at the boneyard."

Molly steps slowly towards him, "how did Dennison get you David." Her voice gentle, filled with empathy.

"I'm special. Cory said so. He likes me. Wants to keep me real close. I am his prince. His special prince."

"Does Willie and Boozer ever get jealous of you?"

"Well," David tilted his head, "well, I don't know. I mean, it doesn't make sense for them to be jealous of me. They are so much smarter than me. They don't have a lisp, but they have to do more stuff for Cory than me. I just lie there," David points to the second bedroom where a twin bed is positioned under a window. A body slumped in it.

"You see, I am free to do as I please."

Molly backed out of the hallway and weaves herself between the 1960's décor furniture and approaches the window. She peers out and then back at David. "What year is it?"

"Well, that's a ridiculous question. It is 1970."

"Come here."

David glides over to her. His eyes, blue and naive, a wave of blonde hair falls and covers his right eye, a pale hand brushed it back. "Look outside David. Can you see outside?"

David peeks between the dark shades of the curtain. For the first time since he had been with Dennison, he looks out with purpose. Before it was out of urgency to grab someone's attention. Anyone. Now, he looks out with a new mission. A new perspective. His eyes, fall on the freshly paved sidewalk, he sees a young man carrying a white bag that said Thank You on it, he is talking into something that he holds close to his face, he stops and looks up at what appeared to be a new three-story townhouse where he puts the foreign talking mechanism in his back pocket and swiftly runs up the stairs. On the left of the new building, he sees a store, one he never recognized before, a crowd of young teens leaning on cars that he did not recognize. His ears are ambushed with laughter and sounds with a strange beat vibrates down the streets along with a combination of loud talking and rhythm bouncing along with it. To the left of a new building, more construction, a sign reading, now leasing, upscale townhomes for an affordable price.

David's voice faltered, "I don't understand, why do things look so different?"

"I think you are stuck in a time loop David." She looks back into the living room. "This isn't my furniture. This is not my house."

"I know, this is Cory's place."

"David, it is not 1970."

David tilted his head, puzzled, "What do you mean?"

"It is 2001. You've been gone since 1970."

"No, what are you saying. I don't understand."

"How many times have you seen the same image of Dennison killing other boys? Listening particularly to the cries of Tommy and Tammy. Willie killing Dennison himself. David, you are trapped here. I think if you would tell me your story, it could help set you free."

David put his hands to his ears, "no, no, no. Cory loved me. I am special. That is why he kept me. I don't like boys the way he does, but he takes good care of me. He's still here. You have seen him. I know you have. Stop it with these words. Willie shooting Dennison. That is not real. It is impossible to bring Cory down. Impossible."

"Listen to me David. You are right. Dennison is here but not in the way that you think. It was all over the news. It happened in the summer of 1973. Willie shot Dennison right there in that hallway. Molly filters through from the window to the hallway. The storage shed, the woods, the beach in Port Arthur, they found the bodies. Many, many bodies. Willie and Boozer led authorities to them after Dennison got shot. The boys that you saw buried." Molly's voice softens, "the boys that died. Killed by Dennison, or Willie or maybe Boozer. I'm not sure of the full extent of Boozer's involvement, but I intend to find out."

"You're wrong. It can't be 2001. Look at me, I am still young, Willie and Boozer are still young. Teenagers. Younger than me. Cory is kind of old but not really. Not compared to my grandma. He is still 33 or 34 he never gives a direct answer. And why am I still here if it is 2001?"

Molly slowly moves herself to the doorway of the guestroom where David lays. "Look."

"It's me."

"How can it be you, if you are standing right in front of me? Why do you keep coming back to this place when you watch the bodies get buried? Why can't you run then? When you are in the woods, or the storage shed? Why?"

David moves past her, into the bedroom and stands over the slumped body. "I'm just sleeping."

"You're in a time loop."

"No, because you are here. Why would you be here?"

"I'm not sure, something happens when I go to sleep. I slip into this time period kind of like a paranormal dream. But I know that this isn't real. That I will wake up."

"Are you so sure of that." A wicked voice boasts from behind. Molly and David quickly turn around to face the interruption. Cory Dennison stands behind them, six foot, big and broad-shouldered. Thick black hair with unmanicured sideburns. "I'm just the friendly Candy Man. Children love me. Mommies love me. They trust me with their little boys." He turns to David, "No my Prince, you know I couldn't do those awful things that she says. I have a girlfriend, she loves me. Even her babies call me Daddy. I don't even lose my temper now do I."

"What's wrong with me. Why am I just lying there like that?"

"You're just resting. Waiting for play time again. Don't you want to play with your old friend Cory."

"Where is Willie and Boozer?"

"In jail," Molly stammered, trying to not show fear."

Simultaneously "They're out running errands for me."

"No, don't believe him. He used them too. He used them to find other boys. To lure them back here. He would give them beer and pot. You know this. You more or less have told me, and what you didn't tell me, old newspapers have filled in the blanks. Dennison tricked you, just like he tricked so many others. He never intended to help you find Jeremy or to let you go back home. He knew that you wanted to help your friend find his son and he took advantage of that." Her eyes soften, "Jeremy was already dead."

"Don't listen to that cow. She'd be better off dead. Just like you."

"David, listen to me. He tortured those boys. He would strip them down, bound their mouths tie a cord or rope around their neck before handcuffing them to that plywood that you have seen in his bedroom. He did awful things to them David. He did awful things to you."

David looked down again at his image. Bending down to see his body up close, he sees the bruising around his neck, his body cold, his eyes opened but empty. He lets out a whimper, "I'm dead. I'm really dead."

"Willie and Boozer confessed to everything. They told the authorities about the friends that trusted them, who they brought to Dennison. Willie even brought somebody that was his best friend from early childhood knowing what that monster had in store for him." Molly's voice got harsher as she points to Dennison, looking at him straight in the eyes." If that beast did not kill the human surprise bestowed on him, then he would get one of the boys to do it. Watching and laughing. Then they would take the bodies to one of his private cemeteries. He turned them into vicious sadist monsters, and he wanted you to become one too." Molly clenched her fists and walked over towards Dennison. "But David was too sweet for that wasn't he. He would never do your bidding and you knew it too. So, after you tortured him, you killed him. Strangled him yourself, didn't you? Then you kept his body, like a trophy for God knows how long, doing god knows what."

"She doesn't know what she is talking about." Dennison cocked his head toward David. "Tell her my Prince, tell her how you liked it."

David began to cry, "no, no, no, I don't. I never liked it. I want to go home. I want to see my mom and Ralph. I don't want to be here anymore."

"Awe is the little prince going to cry?"

"Leave him alone." Molly shouted and rushed after him. "You evil son-of-a-bitch. I read about what you did. The glass rods, the sex toys, you would make them do things to you and you would do things to them. You are nothing but a sick rapist. A rapist and a murderer." Molly ran through him, stumbling on the décor of 2001, waking up in bed.

Getting up, she sees that it is dusk, she pulls herself up and runs to her computer. Got to get it out. She says to herself. I've got to get it out before I lose it. Opening it up, the computer screams flickers, then flashes before steadily coming alive. Molly rapidly begins to type. Her dream, vision, premonition or whatever it was, ignoring the pinch in her stomach, the cramp in her right side, the blood dripping down her leg.

42

2001

For three days, Molly hardly left her computer. Normally she does intensive research when writing pieces involving crime or anything historical but, this article was different. The story came to her. The words spun together in her mind and flew out through her fingertips with little thought. Occasionally she would feel the pang of hunger, the twitch to go to the bathroom, the noticeable drainage of her body. Her menstrual cycle started back up again…weeks before it should have. The thought of I need a doctor, never drifted into her mind. At one point she folded up a towel and sat on it. Dark blue, camouflage for a decaying uterus. The phone rang. Several times. Her mother, Billy even Eddie a few times. But they went unanswered. As well as her Facebook and Myspace messages. Her mind was too busy. Wanting to get every word out. Truth, demented. David's story. Dennison's story regardless of how torrid it is.

A knock sounds at the door. Molly ignores it. The knock sounds louder. Knock, Knock, Knock. Again, she ignores it. Two minutes pass, the knock turns into a pound. Bam, Bam, Bam. What the hell!

Still sticking to the towel, she peels it away from her, body aching, she pulls herself up and goes to the door. Billy is standing there. Looking larger than normal. A red Magellan shirt, wranglers a camo hat. His beard looking thicker than usual, a streak of gray on the side she sees him through the window. She never noticed that before. "Just a minute," she hollers as she straitens out her maxi skirt, blood on the back and the middle of the front. She opens the door. "Come in, I just have to run to the back for a moment." She tries to move quickly hoping to escape Billy's gaze onto her stained skirt.

She makes it quickly to the bedroom speaking while working through her embarrassment. "What's going on?" Molly asked breathlessly.

"Been trying to get a hold of you with no luck. Your mom even called Eddie at the paper." While Billy speaks, Molly cleans herself with a washrag before changing into fresh clothes. "I guess you can consider this a welfare check."

"My welfare is fine," Molly hollers back as she slips on an olive-green maxi dress, flattering to her complexion but loose enough to hide that she's a mess. I need a doctor. "Just getting some pages done. Working on a story for Eddie."

"So, I heard. About Dennison. I tell you Molly, you got to get the hell out of this house. The bad vibes are taking over you." Billy's eyes roll around the house, worried that he will offend it. "When was the last time you ate? You look pale."

Molly comes out, smiles "I'm fine. I have had a revelation though, but I don't think you will believe me."

"At this point, I think I would believe anything."

"Dennison, he was a bad man. There is no denying that. He was also a gay person in a homophobic world. On top of that he had fantasies of torture and murder."

"Yes, I know the story."

Molly drops her shoulders and goes to the pantry pulling out a box of Cheezeits. "Listen to me. I know we know all of that. But we all have some sort of weird fetish that we hide from the world."

"Really?" Billy flirts leaning down on the counter. "What is your fetish?"

"Okay, most of us do. Dennison, however, he may not have acted on anything if he wasn't influenced by some kind of greater power. Willie and Boozer too for that matter."

"Okay, I don't follow. I know that Willie and Boozer acted out because of Dennison but what triggered him."

"Dennison lived at 4646 Durant Street in the Heights when he first began luring kids when he worked at his mom's candy shop."

"Okay,"

"Well, I did a little digging in history on that address, and it too has a violent pass. Well at least the land does. Three prostitutes were murdered there in the sixties and the crime went unsolved."

"Okay, but that is a different scenario than with Dennison. Besides, that isn't farfetched. Houston is not really considered safe you know. Even in the sixties and if they are prostitutes, well you know… they are asking for trouble."

"Do not be so judgmental. Besides, it wasn't that bad back then. Anyway, you are missing my point. Perhaps whatever influenced the murder of those women also influenced Dennison." Molly looks at Billy, feeling crazy but kept on going with her theory. "Maybe Dennison was possessed or haunted."

"What, by a demon or something. You are watching too much late-night horror movies."

"No, listen to me." Molly goes over to the couch and sits down. "Spirit possession is more common than people realize. Why would the Catholic church authorize exorcisms if it wasn't?"

"Dennison probably had a shitty life with a shitty upbringing. Besides, same-sex attraction was not as widely accepted as it is now."

"Yeah, well most of us has had some sort of shitty trauma that happens, and we don't all become serial killers. I think that someone or something influenced him to become the sadistic killer that he became." Billy looked at her with a concerned silence. "Think about it Billy. A demon will focus on the most vulnerable. The weak or the desperate. Dennison had to be desperate. He was a gay person kicked out of the army and hated by his dad. He had desires for younger boys. Children. You don't think a demon would want to feast on that."

"Sounds like you watched the Exorcist one too many times. I don't think you can convince me he was possessed. I believe that he was born pure evil. Good riddance to him and the boys that helped him. I wish those two here dead rotting in hell too."

"Dennison had talents. Even if nobody wants to recognize them. He had charm. A type of charisma that attracted the kids to him."

"He had candy, pot, and beer. I think that was his charm."

"Yes, but even the feeblest does not necessarily accept that from just anyone. A demon gets a perverse joy from igniting pain into others."

"Yeah, but he was born evil. I am sure of it. Maybe he was the demon. A human demon."

"Billy, you heard the voices in here too. They are not human. Besides, do you think a newborn can be born evil. How is that more plausible than a partial possession where a person's mind is controlled by a malevolent entity. Something that would change emotions and behavior. Something to make a person feel extreme hatred, have tantrums or excessive violent outbursts. Maybe something that would encourage wicked fascination."

"Well, I think the devil made me do it defense has been tried and not worked. If it did, everyone would do it. And I mean everyone. If we start throwing out ideas that action is not free will than the court are going to be bogged down with all sorts of absurd crime. Seriously, Molly, you can't publish stuff like you are suggesting. I don't think Eddi would go for it anyway."

"So, you don't think it is possible that somebody's rational judgement could be manipulated by outside forces? Think about it. You even said you saw stories on the Travel channel how entities messed with people's mindset. Couples driven to divorce, violent outbursts in an otherwise pleasant household. The entity trapped in the house stirred that up. You can't sit here and tell me that there is not some sort of interference in these relationships."

"Yes, I can. Unless somebody has multiple personality disorder or something like that, I believe that people that are making such allegations that you are suggesting are full of shit and will make any excuse necessary to avoid taking accountability. Dennison himself, was able to keep a job with the utility company, hold down a steady relationship and make his neighbors think he is an all-around, well-adjusted nice guy only to find the cops, and the news media surrounding their house one day telling them otherwise."

"He fooled them all. How did he get away with it for so long? How were his true colors not seen by all the close neighbors?"

"Because serial killers are like that. Sneaky. Look at Ted Bundy. Do you think he was possessed as well?"

"No, I don't smartass," Billy started to speak by Molly held her hand up, "because even though what he did was horrible, he didn't keep the victims. Toy with them by torturing and letting his victims know that they are going to die."

"I know the story." Billy said solemnly, shifting his position.

Molly sighed. "Look, I don't mean to be insensitive. I am just looking for an explanation."

"And pinning the crimes on a demon is your explanation. Have you ever thought that Dennison was the demon, and he manipulated those poor boys?"

"A few minutes ago, you were cursing them to rot in hell."

"Well, I'm sorry that I am so confused. It is weird to me how people, even naïve teens can be so easily manipulated to commit such horrid acts."

"Unless you are a pro at it."

"So, you think that he did it before. Manipulated other people to commit acts and it just never surfaced. What kind of research are you doing?"

"No, what I am saying is the entity that he picked up in the Heights, the one that followed him here; that is still here, with him in this house guided him and used him as a host to pull these other boys in."

"So, we are back at the devil made me do it defense again." As Billy spoke, the lights flickered, and scratching could be heard in the walls."

"Do you hear that?"

"What the rodents."

"You think you can explain everything, but can you? I mean, isn't your explanations mere excuses to dismiss the possibilities that exist outside of this world."

"Look, I wouldn't live here. Hell, I don't even like being in here."

"Then go. If you are not going to listen to me, just go." Molly's frustration was rising, her stomach cramped and sweat prickled her brow."

Billy's voice softens, he moves closer to her and makes an awkward attempt to snuggle with her, "Look Molly, I believe that there is something here. I mean, I can't deny it. I've experienced it. I don't like this place. I think it might be a good idea for you to move in with me for a while. You know get you out of this place, and I can tell you are still not feeling well." He looks up and around, "I'm not sure if demons or ghosts or whatever is here is capable of practical reasoning, but I do believe that in certain circumstances that a body can be inhabited by another foreign being although I am not sure what you would define it as. And if I acknowledge that, then I must acknowledge that for the weakest of souls the thing inhabiting could possibly control the individual into doing God awful things, including torture and murder. Hell, for all I know, Hitler was possessed. I mean, he did convince an entire army to follow his orders. So maybe, just maybe, Dennison was able to use the same thing over those boys." As Billy spoke, the lights flickered again, Molly's computer began to hum, and her head turned to see the monitor flickering.

"Ah crap!" Molly hollered as she stumbled to the computer.

"It's probably going to sleep. It's been idling for a while."

"I have days of work on there. Research that I have done. I really am coming to a breakthrough with this case."

"Molly, this case is solved. It is almost thirty years old; Dennison is dead, Boozer and Willie are serving life sentences." As Billy spoke, Molly fumbled with the monitor, pounded on the keyboard. The screen flickered before it turned off completely. A quiet harsh laughter sounded in her mind.

"That bastard. He did this."

"Who, Dennison or your demon."

"No, no, no," Molly cries. "I have been working so hard I had a breakthrough." She looks up into the air, "you bastard!"

"Molly, pack a bag. Come with me. If you don't want to stay at my house, we can get a place in Galveston. Breakfast on the beach, doesn't that sound nice. I'll bring my laptop. You can work on that and try and recreate your work."

Molly nods, she pulls out a USB from the side of her computer. "I have most of it saved on this. Only today's work will be missing. I can make it work."

Billy looks at her as she moves about the room. "Have you been sleeping, okay?"

Molly nods, "I've been too anxious. I want to get this story over with. Somehow, I feel like if I write it than it can truly end."

Billy looks up, and then around, "maybe for you, but not for the next person that moves in here. I swear, they need to tear this place down." Then looking back at Molly with a smile, "can I help you pack."

"Well, I wasn't too keen on going back to your dingy place, but a Galveston get away does sound nice."

"Then it is a plan. How about you start packing and I will book us a room. Tremont okay."

"Yes, I have always wanted to stay there." Feeling cramps, "do you mind if I take a shower. I am still not completely healed, and I am embarrassed…"

"Go ahead," Billy waves his hand as he pulls out a phone book. "Take your time. Check in isn't until three anyway."

Molly smiled, looked at him for a moment feeling an overwhelming feeling of affection for him before she turned and padded off to the bathroom.

As Billy is on the phone, he is distracted by a shadow looming in the hallway. He mechanically turns his body away from it, deliberately ignoring it, but despite his stubbornness, it sneaks up on him. After the call, he fiddles with his phone, prevents himself from looking up much like someone sitting alone in a restaurant not wanting to be bothered. But he cannot shut out the voice.

"Ah, Billy boy. You think you are the hero. Take her away. That awful cow. But she has to come back. She has to face me. And when she does, she will die. Die just like Charlie. And there is nothing that your chubby little fingers can do about it."

Fuck you, fuck you, Billy chants softly. The thing laughs. "Do you even know who you are talking to. Am I Dennison or am I, a demon? Maybe I am Satan himself. Wouldn't that be a hoot. Aren't you afraid Billy boy? Aren't you afraid that you will be next? You will be the next one trapped in my web. Perhaps, I will let you do my bidding. Let you see how easy it is for one to be manipulated. How you will not be able to control your own actions. I just might put you in charge of killing Molly. Wouldn't that be fun."

"Molly, do you need any help in there?"

Kill Her! Kill Her! Kill Her!

Molly had just stepped out of the shower and was drying off. "My suitcases are in the closet in the spare bedroom. The one closest to my room. Do you mind getting them out for me? I just need the small one."

Billy gets up and strides to the room, "sure," he deliberately hollers aloud, tying to cover the sound of laughter. He walks in, his eyes fall onto the image of a slumped body on the bed. He blinks twice and it is gone. He steadily opens the closet, pulls down a suitcase and to the left he notices a piece of plywood, and the image of a young man, stripped naked, blood coming out of his mouth, pleading in a soft whimpering tone. Billy blinks his eyes again, the image is gone, but as he walks his boots make crinkling sound on a carpet of thick plastic. It is not there. It is not there. Billy repeats in his head. The plastic is gone, and Molly is peeking into the room.

"The place really does give you the webeye jibes doesn't it."

"Let's just say, I can't wait for you to move out of it."

"Speaking of which, do you think it would be too far to drive from Galveston to here on a regular basis?"

"Why you ask?"

"I don't know," Molly says over her shoulder as she rummages through her closet, pulling out jeans and a couple of nice tops. "I feel like that I would like to live on the island. Well, minus the hurricanes that is."

"You learn to adapt. They literally have tax free day sales on hurricane supplies. It would be neat to have a place on the beach."

"Or the strand maybe." Molly starts packing when the lights flicker. "You know, when I first moved in, I thought that was an electrical issue. Waiting for the place to catch fire each time I flicked a light switch. Now I'm not so sure."

"Molly, do you think," Billy paused, "never mind."

"I hate it when people do that. Just say it, what do I think."

"I'd rather ask you in the car."

"Why, you afraid the house will react. See, you do think that I am on to something." Molly bends over in a cramp. She stumbles and pulls out a prescription of 800 mg ibuprofen.

"You, okay?"

"Not sure. Do you think that an evil being can attack a person's bodily organs?"

"Are you sure you want to go? We can go back to my place."

"No, I want to go and spend time in Galveston. Even it if is just hanging around the hotel. I am sure once I am up and going, I will be fine. Besides, I need to place to write my article without interference." A wicked laughter shakes her head.

"Well, maybe they can cause you to have a virus or something. Hell, you may be able to explain the great plagues of the world."

"Maybe," Molly grasps her USB that she managed to keep within her eye contact even in the shower. She drops it in a black tattered coin sack and then deposits it in her purse. She looks up, "gotta make sure that I got that." Then she looks around, "shall I pack some snacks."

"Nah," Billy says nervously, "we gotta stop off at my place so I can pack a few things." Noting Molly's unease, "you can lay down there if you want. It won't take me long. It is only about 45 minutes from here, once we get checked in, we can go and have a nice dinner. What do you think? Salt Grass or Rionda's."

"They both sound good. I think though I would prefer Italian." She moves closer to Billy and lets him put his arm around her.

"You got enough feminine products?"

"What they don't have drugstores there." Billy blushed, "don't worry, I'll be fine. No trips to the emergency room this time around. In fact, I think once we leave, my exhaustion and moodiness will disappear."

43

The Pied Piper's Prince

I do not understand why I must be kept here. I have done nobody any harm. I see Cory for what he is. He never offered up a safe place for teens to come. He offered up a place to get drunk, get high. A place to be tortured in unimaginable ways and then to die. He didn't lie about one thing though. Jeremey was here. He did get invited in. But I know he did not come for the beer or to smoke that nasty stuff. Jeremy is a good kid. A sweet kid that loved his mother and his daddy and his dog. He was my friend, even though he was young. He never made fun of the way I talked or how I got confused on things. Even simple things that Ralph said that I should know and get, Jeremy, he never made fun of me.

Cory, I see it now, he is not my friend. He is touched in the head with madness, or a mental disorder or something. My grandmother says that there were some people that existed in the world where something just wasn't right with them. She'd say that some people got their brains all jumbled up. Not in the smarts kind of way like me, but in the kindness kind of way. Grandma use to say there was different kind of smarts. Now I remember teachers talking to us kids in class when they would have us take these weird learning quizzes. I asked grandma about those, but she said the teachers in school have it all wrong. That the smarts really live in your head and your heart. She said it was okay that the smarts in my head was off balance because I could still live a good life, but that when the smarts in your heart is messed up, wired wrong as she would say, then there was a whole mess of trouble. That is when people act bad and don't care about it. It doesn't bother them. Grandma said that was real bad. Cory is like that. He acts bad and it doesn't bother them. He is like the big bad wolf in the woods.

The scariest thing about Cory though is that you don't know he is bad until it is too late. My mom likes him. So does Benny and Rose. So does Jeremy; or at least they did. I am so confused right now. Things don't seem right. The couch. I am so confused about the couch. Most of the time it is a brown and orange striped looking thing. Rough, covered with dog hair, spilt beer and smells of weed and dirty old socks. But other times, the couch is mauve, clean and new. A light smell of fragrance like a flower, but spicy kind of. Other things sometimes looked different too. I like it though because I don't see the boards or hear the screams. But I still see myself slumped on a bed in the spare bedroom. The one that Molly uses for storage. The one where she has a full-length mirror attached to a wall. I can't see myself in it though.

Molly, I don't really know how I know her. I don't really know how she came into my life but sometimes she is there and sometimes she is not. It's strange, but I do feel like I can trust her. I have to because with Cory walking around here, you never know what kind of temper you gonna find him in. I wondered if Jeremy ever figured out that he was bad. Did Cory catch him by surprise or did he have time to think about it. Process it, like mom would say. I don't know what is worse. Knowing that you are going to die and to be prepared for it, where you got to think about death and whisper out a few last goodbyes even if there is no one or nothing to hear it but the wind or die quickly. The life bleeds out of you instantly. It goes both ways around here. Usually with Willie, it is a bang and then you're gone. With Cory, there is time. Time to think, to look at Cory strait in the eyes as he holds your throat so tight, and he laughs at you while he does it. His nasty sloppy body on top of yours. You feel so tiny and helpless, you can't scream out because the pressure on your throat, you can't swallow, and his weight is too big to push you off. So, all you can do is plead with him through your eyes as you look up into his and…oh my God…

44

Within the Vale

"Why am I here?"

Molly opens her eyes and looks up at David. No longer fearing him, she sits up. "What?"

"Why am I here?"

Molly squinted her eyes in confusion. She tilts her head, puzzled she asks, "don't you know?"

David shakes his head. Although Molly can see him better, make out his structure, his facial features, he is still transparent to her. As she looks at him, she sees a dark shadow, not as clear to her, behind him. Slowly she begins to speak. Reciting notes, she found in her research.

"Your mother loves you so much. Every day, she would go to Strawberry Park, a place that you loved to play. A place where you would love to feed the ducks. She uses this plastic bucket, the one that you used when you were a kid, and she would take you to Sylvan beach when you wanted to collect shells. She throws old bread in the bucket that she kept on the kitchen counter, and she would drive to the park and find a bench close to where the ducks are, and she would feed them. Just like you liked to do when you were younger. You would walk around the park, sometimes run because you wanted to try out for track. That was when the park was first built before it got polluted. She said that when she would feed the ducks, she felt like you were with her in some kind of way. Your brother goes there now sometimes. He brings his son there."

Emotion welled up in Molly, "I'm so sorry for them. Ralph named his son David, after you."

David began shaking his head back and forth, putting his hands over his ears. "No, no, no," he stuttered. "That is not real. I am here. Cory kept me. He will let me go one day if I am really good and do what he says."

"One year, on the anniversary of Dennison's death, a news reporter interviewed Ralph. It was hard on him because your mother had just died."

"No, you lie. My mother is alive, and she is waiting for me."

Molly began to cry. "No David, Ralph said that one day you walked up to your mother, kissed her on the cheek and told her that you loved her, then you ruffled Ralph's hair, and walked out the door and was never seen again."

"No! I went to look for Jeremy, and then I saw Cory..." David stuttering is more evident. A heavy darkness clouds over him, "and then I saw Cory and he told me that Jeremy was at his house and that I could come talk to him and maybe convince him to go home." He began to sputter out his words, shaking. He pauses as an ominous voice echoes.

"Go ahead you limp dick. Tell her the story."

"This isn't happening."

Molly's voice grows louder, "your mom called all your friends, they called Benny even though he was going through his own crisis, there were people from all over the neighborhood, driving in their cars, roaming all the streets and local restaurants. They even called the hospitals to see if you were admitted but nobody knew where you are."

Molly stands, when she hears more of the wicked laughter. She steps aside David and walks towards it. "You are nothing but a sick son-of-a-bitch. You were out there looking for them too. Pretending to be all concern when the entire time you his body was decomposing in your bedroom."

"No, Cory, tell her it isn't true."

"You even had Boozer, rewrite a fake his note about him going to Austin to try and find work. You stupid fuck. The kid can barely write, and you fake a note. There was no way he would have left his mother and his little brother."

"I didn't leave! I went to look for Jeremy and… and…"

"And you never came home." Dennison's shape suddenly became clearer to Molly.

Molly turns back to David. "It wasn't just the park either. She fixed her hours so that she could come home early every day. She would wait on the stoop, pace the sidewalk, go through the house and walked the border of the chain-link fence that surrounded the edge of your yard. She even would wait by the mailbox for the mail carrier even though Ralph told her there was no way you could have written that note or any note."

"Ahh. Your poor mother." Dennison hissed. "Waiting for a letter that would never come, every sound she heard at night, she jumps out of her bed and rushed to the door, praying it was you. Oh, how she wanted to just hug your unmasculine body just one last time. Oh, the poor old hag, that couldn't possibly be good for her heart disease."

"What's wrong with her heart?"

"Nothing anymore."

"Shut up Dennison!" Molly's voice was strong and bold. She stepped closer to Dennison. "You are nothing. Nobody cares about you. Nobody visits your grave and mourns for the likes of you. You aren't even interesting enough to bring out the true crime novelist to hear your story."

Dennison hisses at Molly and with a supernatural strength he hurls at her, knocking her against the wall. Molly struggles to get up but laughs at her pain. "You're forgotten. Lost in the textbooks, replaced by stronger, better looking and more confident killers than you. All that's left is this disgusting piece of a house. And I wouldn't be surprised if it is torn down and replaced with cute little bungalows and offices, who don't even give a crap about the likes of you." Laughing louder, "you won't even have a decent place to haunt now, will you?" Marching up closer to him. "Some people don't even believe you ever existed. They think you are just some weird, bizarre urban legend that died in the dusk of Grimm tales and exploited news media."

"What about me? Does anyone know about me?" David looks around helplessly, he darts passed Molly and Dennison, past the shadows of memories in the hallway and lunges himself into the spare bedroom. Molly stumbles behind him, Dennison laughs and the image around the room rotates as if they were in a kaleidoscope. First it seemed like snapshots, then the room moved, titled, rotated again and then rested on a scene. One that Molly and David could not enter but only view as silent observers.

David, very much alive, naked on a board, traces of blood outlines his wrists as he pulls at the handcuffs that hold him down. Dennison over him, sitting on him, taking one hand he wraps it around his neck. Molly looks sideways at David standing beside her, his mouth gapes open, his eyes wide as Dennison holds him down, strangling him. David sees his own legs kicking up, shaking his arms give another tug at the handcuffs and then his legs drop, his arms drop, his hands open, limp.

A live version of Dennison gets up. A voice is heard from down the hallway. "Where do you want us to stash him at?"

"Nowhere yet," Dennison answers. "I like this one a bit. Let's keep the prince around for a while. I can still play with him until he starts to smell."

"I don't understand, I thought you liked me. I thought I was special."

"Ahh come on. I buried you in the backyard under the shed." Molly's head jerked up.

"What?"

45

2001

Two weeks had passed since Billy and Molly got back from Galveston and she was already looking forward to going back. Even in the daylight, the house seemed dingy and gray. It had been a few days since she heard from David and for an odd reason, she felt concern. She also had not heard from Dennison, but that was a good thing. There were times that she heard or at least she thought she heard sounds echoing form the corners of the room. Heckles, snorts and occasional growls. She did her best to tune them out although it was hard not to be rattled by them, especially when they came at night.

Eddie loved Molly's story as it stirred up interest in the community causing concerned citizens to request a renewal of the case in hopes of finding more bodies and answer more questions. There were still several aging parents who were convinced that their son was a victim of Dennison's or that the boys that helped him had knowledge of the boy's whereabouts. Reporters began visiting the Mark Stiles unit prison in Jefferson County to visit the two thugs. Boozer turned down interview invitations but Willie wouldn't shut up. He embellished his role, making himself out to be the mastermind. The various cemetery's that Dennison had become despicable tourist cites inviting search organizations with advanced equipment to excavate the areas in search of bodies and a politician even petition the crime lab to run some of the cold cases against DNA samples. A technique that was not available in the seventies. There were still a couple of boxes of decayed remains that did nothing but gather dust in cardboard boxes. A tooth, a femur, not a full set of remains but enough that had yet deteriorated so bad that a clear identification could not be made. Renewed hope excited Eddie as paper sales rose to a high that it had not seen in years which influenced his devotion to bringing closure to the victims' families. He set up a phone line for relatives to contact the paper with a name and a date, which he would then personally advocate for a forensics unit to make a connection between family and victim. There were even a few families who thought they had buried their child who requested that bodies be exhumed and have a new analysis ran thinking that it was not their son in the coffin but somebody else's.

The story brought ignited compassion from the bank that Molly rented the house from. They agreed to allow the backyard to be dug up.

"Sir, I think it would put the neighborhood at ease. Maybe they would stop poking around here if they thought there were no bodies here." Molly said to him as she was pointing to the backhoe to begin in the area where a storage shed once stood in 1973. Satisfied that the hired labor was going to dig in the right area, she walks back into the house and decides to call Billy.

"How are you feeling?"

"Weak but the doctor gave me more medicine. He says though that I need to either have a baby or a hysterectomy." Molly waits as there is a strong silence on the other end.

"So, what are you saying? You want a baby?"

"This isn't the time in my life that I would want one. But I guess I will never have one because the bleeding only stops in intervals and every time it starts back up again it gets worse."

"You did good in Galveston." Billy said with a laugh.

Molly closes her eyes and dreamily says, "I did have a wonderful time."

"You know, it is expensive to live there."

"I know," Molly's voice dropped. "I've been checking. At least where I want to live. I was checking out this cool place by that big cemetery that we took a ghost tour of."

"I would think you had your fill of cemetery's. Aren't they digging your yard up now?"

"Yea, and I am afraid to look."

"Well, this may be too soon to bring this up, but we do seem to mesh well."

Molly smiled as Billy talked to her, "maybe we should consider living together. My lease is coming up at the end of December and I would be willing to look at that place you are interested in. Maybe with both of our paychecks we could get the place together."

"Mr. Mackey, are you asking me to move in with you?"

Billy let out a laugh. "I guess I am." As Molly listened to Billy talk about how they could build a nice life in Galveston, she gets up and goes to her computer which is opened to her newspaper email account. She nearly drops the phone when she sees the email pop up in response to hers, Is David your brother?

"Billy." Molly interrupts him in mid-sentence. "Let's plan to go look at it. I'll call the realtor. I think it is a lease to buy kind of deal. I just got to go now."

"Did they find something in the digging?"

"I don't know. But I heard from Ralph."

"Wait, the brother of your ghost?"

"Stop calling him my ghost."

"Well, he is, isn't he?"

"Yeah, I guess, but then again, this proves he is real." Molly opened the email as they spoke.

David was working for Benny at his wreck yard at the time. He didn't make much, but he liked to go there, and our mom thought it was good for him. That is how he became friends with Benny and the rest of the family. Mom knew Cory Dennison's mother because she was working at a hair salon in the Heights when they opened a candy shop. She'd bring sweets home. I was just a baby at the time, but David was about nine or ten and he would go over there because they were always giving kids sweets and stuff. Mom loved the divinity and David like the pecan chewie's. She talked about those for years. Anyway, David would go over there, and she never thought anything of it because there were several kids that would go there after school. He even turned an office into a game room in the back of the factory. So, mom felt safe with David hanging out there even though he always said he didn't know him well because he didn't talk much. Mom felt like it was easier to just send him there instead of having him under her feet at the salon. We moved to Pasadena in 1970 and mom was thrilled when she found out that Dennison was moving into his dad's old house nearby. She thought having a male role model around would be a blessing.

This is hard to write about. Do mind giving me a call?

Molly reread the letter three or four times before her trembling fingers picked up her cell phone and dialed the number.

"Hello." The voice on the phone was friendly and cheerful.

"Yes, Mr. Prince, I'm Molly Matthews."

"Well, hello again. I am happy to hear from you. Would you like to meet for coffee? I can come to Pasadena. Is that Starbucks on Spencer next to the Planet Fitness still there?"

46

The Pied Piper's Prince

Things are clearer now. And I don't like it. I sit at the window more now and watch the world outside move. Sometimes it seems like it is moving in circles. Things changing and the odd-looking cars, the music, the people walking fast. Everyone always seems to be in a hurry. Completely unaware that I am watching. Of if they do know I am here, they don't care. A faceless observer in the window watching them, the construction, the machines, the cars, the people. So different but always the same. In a rush.

I ignore Cory now when he calls my name. I won't be his little prince anymore. All those people he fooled. I should have listened when Mom suggested that I should not hang around Cory so much and that I should find friends my own age. But I really didn't talk to him when I worked at Benny's Boneyard. She always liked him until she one of her boyfriend's Jake questioned his intentions. He said that Cory seemed odd to him and that it wasn't right for a grown man to want so many boys around. I remember asking her why, she didn't have a problem when he worked at the candy place. She was even happy when he moved to Pasadena. Said it would be nice to have him around. Well, it was nice until Jake got in the picture and questioned things. I wish I would have listened to him. He did try and be nice to me, but I wouldn't have anything to do with him. Jake and my mom were engaged when I left. I wonder if they got married. He didn't know I could hear him when he told her that she shouldn't let me go there cuz he was one of those homo people and that it wasn't right for him to have so many little boys around and because I'm slow, I might as well have been a little boy. At first mom ignored him and said that it didn't matter what Cory was because he was good to the children and God loved all of his people regardless of who they liked.

I kind of thought Cory loved me. I thought God loved me. Now, I am not so sure on both. I wish I could apologize to Jake.

47

Within the Vale

"Why were the police here?"

The room was so dark that Molly could barely make out his figure. "David?"

"Yes, why were the police here. Are they going to take Dennison away? Are they going to charge him with what he did to me? Am I gonna get to go home now?"

Molly gets up, exhausted but empathetic towards the pleading ghost's questions. "They found you today. The police found where Dennison put you."

"Wait, what? I'm right here."

Molly gets up, checks her pajama bottoms for blood and then walks to the kitchen. David trailing behind her. "I don't understand."

Molly turns on the light by the back door illuminating the back yard. A backhoe still stands by the pieces of a metal building. Yellow caution tape swirled around wooden pickets marks a hole"

"What's that?"

"It's where they found you."

"That can't be. You went with me to the burial sites. Nobody was buried back there. The other boys buried the others in the woods, at the beach, even in a shed, but nobody was buried here. Nobody."

Molly's voice grows solemn with sympathy, "Dennison did keep you for a while. In that room, just like you seen. On that bed. But..." Molly's voice grows hesitant. "Maybe he put you back there so he could keep you close. Maybe in some sort of sick way he wanted to come and visit you." She reaches to put her hand on his shoulder, his unsolid shoulder…, even in a dream state, her hand falls through.

Tears well up again in David's eyes. "I can't feel your touch." He looks steadily into the backyard, "I can't feel it when it is hot or when it is cold. You make cinnamon buns all the time. I love the smell of cinnamon buns; it always makes me hungry. I can't feel it when I am hungry. I miss being hungry." He swallowed hard, "one time my mother took me to the livestock show at the Houston rodeo. I got to pet a bunny. It was soft and had a little pink nose. I adored that bunny. For weeks afterwards I kept asking mom if I could have one. I told her that I would take care of it and feed it and clean its cage. I wish I could pet a bunny again. Why me? Why did he have to pick me?"

"I am so sorry David. There were many boys. Just like you. Most of them younger than you. As young as twelve.

Sometimes they disappeared while they were out with other friends, family even." Molly's voice drifted. "So many memories stolen. A boy's that didn't have their first kiss, graduation, marriage, children of their own. That didn't get to see adulthood. Get married and have kids." She paused, "David, how old were you when you left with Dennison to get Jeremy?"

"I was twenty."

Molly got quiet, calculating in her head, "49. You would be 49 now." There was a long pause between them, the moonlight seemed to bounce off the backhoe, mocking them. "You walked out of the house and vanished into thin air. That's what your brother said. Thin air."

"You talked to my brother?"

"Yes." She turns and looks at him, "I am meeting with him tomorrow."

"Can I go with you?"

"I don't know, can you leave the house?"

48

2001

Ralph was handsome. Slightly balding with wired rimmed glasses but handsome in a quiet conservative way. Molly felt hesitant in meeting him. Not exactly sure what to say but it didn't matter to Ralph. Over the years, he had become obsessed with his brother's case. He had started a social media support group for family members of the victims and has been hounding the police department for years to keep searching for boys, some who had gone missing as far away as California. Not convinced that Gacy had beaten Dennison's record.

"You know that at the time, the police barely did anything to investigate the disappearance of those boys. Called them runaways. Even David, a guy that had an IQ of 82, was thrown out as a runaway. He had never even left home before. Can you believe that? Said there had to be direct evidence of foul play. How could they find that kind of evidence if he disappeared on the streets?"

"How did you know that Dennison took David?"

"They found Jeremy's remains up at the Rayburn property. David was looking for Jeremy the day that he disappeared. I kept expecting that they would call soon after about David's too." Ralph sighs, "Mom wanted to believe he was still alive. Just lost, but I always knew he was gone. Even before that kid shot Dennison. I knew he was gone." Ralph looks down at his coffee. "Mom fell apart right in front of my eyes. She was so desperate to get him back. She was never quite right after all of that."

"You must have freaked out when the medical examiner's office called you for a DNA sample."

"You got that right." He looks at Molly, "that must have creeped you out, them finding a body in your own backyard."

Molly shrugged her shoulders, looks out the window facing Spencer Street. "Not really, I mean, it is not like it is really my house. I'm hoping to move out soon."

"Can't say that I blame you. They should tear that place down."

"That's what my boyfriend says." She looks at him, "his brother was one of Dennison's victims as well."

"Really, they might have known each other. I mean, Dennison tended to pick up kids around the same areas. So did his heathens."

"Yeah," Molly leans back in her chair, "the boys that could have stopped him, became monsters themselves."

"No kidding," Ralph leans in, "you know, I never believed that David River's or Boozer as he became known, had nothing to do with the murder. I mean, he helped get the kids in, what was in it for him. I think he liked it. I mean, it wasn't like he didn't know what was going to happen to those kids. And the police, well they certainly weren't any help."

"I know, I have been looking into a few of the old cases and there are definitely some inconsistencies that don't add up. Like a kid running away when he was about to go on vacation."

"Yeah, I know about that one. He left money on the dresser too. A kid isn't gonna leave their money behind. I don't care how dumb they are." Ralph takes another drink. "Someone had even reported seeing one of the kids in his GTX. They had his license plate, they could have connected him to the candy factory, the neighborhood, everything and the bastard wasn't even interviewed as a suspect."

Molly could see the anger building in his eyes. "I'm so sorry." Looking around and then back to him, trying to pull her words slowly, "if talking to me is too much for you, I understand. I should probably go."

"No," Ralph reaches out towards her. "I don't really have anyone to talk to about it. With my mom gone and Nancy gets so tired of hearing about it. There are times that I talk about it incessantly."

"Whose Nancy?"

Molly looked up and saw the thin outline of David. She squinted her eyes, "how are you here?"

"I'm sorry."

Molly looks back at Ralph. "I'm so sorry, thought I was hallucinating for a moment." She looked over Ralph's shoulder at David, still standing there curiously looking at the older version of his brother. "Ralph, how did you meet your wife, Nancy."

Ralph smiles back at her. "We met at a rally at UT. I was on my way to the dorm, and I walked right through this group of women, all looking at someone on the podium spilling out a speech on the right to say no to a man." He lets out a laugh, "here I was, in the middle of a mob of angry college girls and all I could think was how beautiful that speaker was. Hell, I was scared to death to ask her out. I found out who she was and what her class schedule was, I conveniently showed up in just the right spots to be seen until I was able to get up the nerve to ask her out. Well, the rest is history. Now here I am, married with a boy of my own." His voice turned distant while he turned his gaze towards the street, whispering, "David would have been a great uncle."

Molly and Ralph sat together in silence looking out at the traffic. Not sure what to say to each other for a long time. Finally, Molly looks at her watch, planning her getaway when Ralph spoke slowly, "you know, I saw that Willie kid once. He was hanging posters at the Long John Silver. You know, the one off Southmore. Hanging it for some poor mother looking for her child. Probably all the while, knowing he was buried in an unmarked grave. He was a rough looking kid. Not sure what girls saw in him. Of course, I was young and knew nothing about girls myself. Guess the kid was too damn stupid to know that he was meant to be a victim himself. I heard that Dennison spent holidays with that kid and his family. Boozer's too for that matter. All the while he trained them both to be monstrous accomplices."

Molly looked at him. In an attempt to play the devil's advocate, she admits, "they were young and stupid. Looking for a way to make quick cash. Dennison offered him that."

"Those boys were his friends. It is bad enough to do that to strangers but to lure in friends. That sick bastard. Sitting at the dinner table with a family one day and then luring a kid to his death the next. Sick."

"You spent a lot of time on your research."

Ralph looks up, "I wonder what David's last moments were like. Was it Dennison himself that took him or one of his disgusting henchmen?"

In a barely audible EVP whisper, David says, "it was him. Cory did it, and all I could think about was my mom and my little brother." The spirit drops his head down, "I guess he is not so little anymore."

Molly put her hand on Ralph's arm. "My gut tells me it was Dennison himself. I think David believed that he was going to help Jeremy but got tricked into going to the home where Dennison and Willie played that handcuff game that you probably read about. Although, Dennison and those awful boys kidnapped and killed several kids, I do believe that it is David who they found buried in the yard." Swallowing hard, "I pray this will bring you closure."

"Tell him that my last thoughts were about him, and mom. Tell him that I never forgot about them and that I always wanted to go home. Tell him that I tried to leave but I couldn't." David's voice grows louder but he is sobbing, "tell him I still want to go home. I still want to be with him and mom in that nasty old house that smells like mold and day-old trash. Tell him that I still love them. I love them so much."

Molly listened to David's soft panicked pleas. "Ralph, I hope you know that David loved you and your mom very much."

"I was kept alive on the plywood for three days because Cory liked me so much. Not like the others where he would cut off their private and do gross stuff with them. He kept me in one piece. He liked me. I was his prince. His incredibly special prince. He told Willie that too. That's why he left my body alone after Cory finally took my breath away. My body stayed in the spare room for three days. Three long days."

Ralph turns in his chair and places his gaze back at Molly. "What provokes a man to do such horrible things. He may have had a lust for those boys, but I think that Willie had a lust for killing. How the hell did he get away with it for so long. So many mothers calling the police, the news, putting up posters. So many and yet there was nobody to connect the dots."

"Things were harder back then. There were no computers, the different departments of the police didn't communicate with each other. Hell, there were no Amber Alerts, community chat rooms. There were barely in-person support groups." Molly leans in, "you know if it wasn't for Willie, there is no predicting how long Dennison would have continued to kill." Leaning back, "he wiped out families. Can't even imagine what would go through those mothers' heads, not just having one son taken but multiple."

"Those boys would go to school or hang around the neighborhood, making it seem like everyone was okay. Acting like they were a tremendous help hanging those posters. What pieces of shit." Ralph started to say more, but his phone rang in his pocket. "Excuse me." Molly drank her coffee, looking around the Starbucks, not paying much attention to Ralph when suddenly in his deep voice, she hears him say, "I see." Ralph's tone snaps her back into focus. She stares at him as she hears him say, "so when can I recover his remains." Molly head feels with a daze as she suddenly realizes that David's ghost was no longer with them. Looking around panickily while Ralph turns ends his call. His face is pale, as he slips it back into his pocket. He tries to take another drink from his empty cup before saying slowly…

"They found him. They found David."

49

The Pied Piper's Prince

One day, my body was just gone. Disappeared, like me. Yet, I was still here. Watching Cory, Willie and Boozer. Sometimes they were in good moods, and they would party, drinking, smoking or sniffing paint spray bottles and stuff like that. You know the things that moms say you should never do cuz they would fry your brain. But then there were other days. Scary days. It was like Cory got all possessed or something lighting up those cigarettes one after another. No matter how many times Willie or Boozer would try to empty those ashtrays, they were always full again in no matter of time.

I watched the whole thing play out time and time again. For a while I thought that I was watching my own experience again cuz it was always the same thing. You see, sometimes Cory's eyes would glaze over. He puffed at those Marlboros, stinking up the room and his voice would get choppy while he made these jerky movements like he was having a seizure or something. Willie would go and say something like, "whatcha needing boss," and then Cory would glare into space and say something like, "I need a new boy. Get someone for me. You know what I like. Like he was ordering off the drive through menu or something. Then the other boys would come back with a kid they lured off the street believing they were coming back to party with them.

I lost count of how many boys that I saw turn into bodies. How they were wrapped up in that thick plastic used to carpet the floor. The sound they made when they were dragged out in the dark of night and buried under the bright lights of the storage shed, or the moonlight by the pond. I know now that I was put into the backyard. Because I am special. Cory liked me and wanted to keep me close.

50

Within the Vale

"He killed them. He killed them all." Dropping his head, "and he killed me too."

"You have been found. Your brother is having what is left of your body cremated. You are free to leave this place. Go and join your mother."

"Ah, do you miss your mommy?"

"Ignore him, David. He is a sick bastard, and you never have to deal with him again."

"What my little prince. You can't move on."

"Shut the fuck up Dennison. Leave him alone. You're dead too you stupid fuck. That kid you used to bring in your prey, he turned on you. How does that feel." Molly no longer feeling fear walked straight up to the shadow of a monster. "That's right. You thought you convinced him to kill that Tammy girl, but you were fooled. You stupid prick, you were fooled. "My god, that must have been a beautiful sight. Willie grabbing the gun and aiming it right at you. Were you scared?

Having that gun aimed right at you. Your right hand threatening to take the life out of you. How did it feel Cory? How did if feel knowing you were going to die."

Molly walked even closer nearing his chest. Her short, stocky frame seemed tiny compared to his, but she didn't care. Suddenly a voluminous voice coming from behind her shook the house.

"This ain't happening any longer. You are killing my friends. You are using me." Then a shot rang out. Then another. Then another. The shadow of Dennison stepped back, and there crumpled on the floor the dough like figure of a naked man slumped over. Molly looks at David, then the shooter and then at the ghost of Dennison.

"You're such a limp dick."

Dennison lurches at her but Molly stands her ground. He falls through her; she laughs and then turns to David and says to him. "You can go home now."

51

2001

"Thank you for letting me a part of this." Molly said slowly, smiling at Ralph then his wife and then to his son.

"We wouldn't be here without out you." Ralph said reassuringly.

Molly looks around the small chapel. "Well, I don't think I want to be remembered as someone you invited to a funeral."

"No," taking a deep breath. "You will be remembered as someone who has brought closure to my family. I don't think that the anger and sadness will ever disappear, but at least we know where David is. I will no longer be kept up at night wondering what happened to him."

"But you had said before that you always known that Dennison killed him."

"This is true," Ralph says while shaking his head, "but now, I have proof, and now David can rest in peace." Ralph hands over a small mason jar to Molly. "I know this isn't much. They were not able to get all of him since so much time has passed. But" Ralph says thoughtfully, "at least the DNA was a true match. There are still families out there not completely sure if they buried their own family member or someone else's child."

"Well, perhaps with all the media coverage that this is getting," Molly nods out the tall narrow window where news cars could be seen parked around the lot, "perhaps they will consider exhuming some of the bodies like family members have asked."

"You know, I have heard that, and I have even a few television reporters leave me messages asking what I thought about the matter, but I say, let the boys lie. God knows where they are, and we have to keep the faith that they are all at peace." Then looking down at the jar of ashes in Molly's clutches, "course I guess that is easy to say, since I know now where my brother is." Swallowing hard, "Thank you for everything. I feel you are family, and I am happy to give you some of his ashes to keep or spread if you like." Molly smiled and Ralph reached in and gave her a hug. "Are you sure about that? You barely know me."

"There is something in my gut that says that he is as much as a part of you as he is of me. Maybe more considering the place and time." Ralph then steps back, brings in his own son, "come on David, let's go."

Molly watched as Ralph and his family walked outside, Ralph shielding his wife and son from the reporters and rushing them to the car. She sat down hoping to wait out the news crew when she heard David's voice behind her. "I can't believe he named him after me. He never forgot me."

"Of course not. People don't forget. They just learn to move on." She looks at him, surprised by how much clearer she could see him. She could make out facial features, the blue in his eyes, the softness of his hair. "Come on, Let's do this."

"Where are we going?"

"To the last place that I know you were truly happy."

Molly found a back way to sneak out and when she got to the parking lot, most of the news trucks were packing up and didn't notice her. She slipped in her red corolla and was able to creep by the roadies without them giving her a second thought. She could not see David in the car, but she felt his presence. She drove by the storage shed, and David whispered. "Number eleven."

"What?" Molly thought.

"Number eleven. They'll find more boys buried under the cement in storage shed eleven. I'm sure they are still there."

"Good to know," Molly thought. "Will figure out a way to get that part of the story known." She eases the car into the parking lot of Strawberry Park. "Do you remember this place," she asked in her thoughts, but David did not respond. That did not sway her. She got out, her black dress flapping in the wind, her scuffed up heels stepping over a curb into a patch of grass that led to a sidewalk that circled the pond where several ducks were playing. She took a seat on a bench facing a synthetic island built in the middle of the water. It is peaceful here, she thought.

"You know, my mom used pills and alcohol to cope with the pain after my dad left. She went a little crazy. She said she was doomed to be alone. I guess she must have really felt that way after I left. I can't even imagine how she dealt with it when she realized that I wasn't coming back. Poor Ralph had to deal with all that pain."

"Yes, well when murders happen, it might as well be a genocide effect. Dennison didn't just kill boys. He killed entire families. The road of destruction that he left was massive."

"You should not go back. To that house that is. With him there and all. You shouldn't be alone there."

Molly smiled at him "You know, I think I can handle it. Besides, I have always wanted to be a BBBA."

"What is a BBBA?"

"That would be my own acronym for Big Beautiful Bad Ass." She notes the confusion on the David's face as once again he began to appear in front of her. "When I was a kid, I use to watch Batman and Robin and well…well, I always had this silly fantasy to be Cat Woman. You know, she was beautiful in her leather suit and irresistible to all the men, yet she could kick all the ass of all the men." She looks up at him, "sounds ridiculous I suppose."

"Not necessarily. I always wanted to be superman. A hero. Somebody that someone could look up too."

Molly looks at him, thoughtfully, "you know," clucking her tongue to the roof of her mouth. "You know David, you really are a hero."

"I don't exactly know what you mean by that."

"The killings that Dennison committed before and after he moved into the house. People that we probably don't even know about and will never know about since the search was halted so long ago, well you must have been inhabiting," thinking carefully about her words, "haunting a house occupied with the devil."

"Do you believe that Cory is the devil"

"No, not exactly, but I know that there is something else there, in that house that inhabits that place and I think that it has attached itself to Dennison long before he ever moved in there. It just exasperated itself there once he was in the home. Knowing that it was his place and that the chance of Dennison moving again was unlikely. It penetrated itself into Dennison mind, which is how he transformed to what people described as a once charming candy man to a colossal monster unleashing his fury on everything and everyone else but him. He hated the fact that he had gay feelings, so he blamed the objects of his affections." She turns towards David.

"But I'm not, not," David stutter begins to return, "I am not like that." He says more slowly.

"It doesn't matter. He wanted to be so called normal. Or at least what normal was seen as in your time. The seventies that is. He wanted to please his mother, get married and have children like a normal man his age, but his feelings and emotions weren't wired that way, so to speak. So, he took boys, and he tortured them, knowing that the same affections that he could have possibly felt towards them would never be returned. That unleased a chain of hate that was fueled by the demon that is also attached to him and now that house or his soul at least."

"Do you really think it is a demon in there with us."

"Yes, I do. Something brought him to madness. To evil. Something now, keeps that house smelling like rotting flesh regardless of what kind of deodorizers and scented candles that I use. But there is no us in the equation anymore. It is time for you my friend to move on."

"We are friends."

"One of the best I have ever had." David smiled at her.

"How will you remember me?"

"The way I know you I suppose."

"As a ghost that haunted you?"

Molly let out a laugh. "No, not really. More like a boy frozen in time, and I don't mean that in a sorrowful way but more in admiration The boy that wanted to be a hero and was."

"But I wasn't able to save Jeremy."

"Oh, there are many ways to be a hero, David. You may not have saved Jeremy, but your presence in that house may have saved others. Those that could sense that there was evil dwelling there. And yet, you stayed, and I imagine I am not the first occupant that you warned."

"Yeah, but nobody would listen to me. Besides most of them left as quickly as they came."

"Scared by history, I'm sure. But nudging yourself in their dreams probably helped."

"Is it really 2001?"

"It is. You have been there a long time. Your old room at your house would have been cleaned out a long time ago. Your brother and your mother had no choice but to move on. I am sure, you mother kept certain mementos as all mothers would do. A lock of hair from your first haircut, a first lost tooth a drawing or report card. But your remains or what is recognizable is in a vase with your brother and here in my hands."

David looks down at the small micro pieces of him transformed into dust. "You don't have to see yourself in that bed anymore. Never again will you have to face the likes of

Cory Dennison or that horrible creature that is attached to him."

"It doesn't seem right to let you go back and face that alone."

Molly moved slightly, feeling a pinch of a cramp. "It will be fine. You have been the hero long enough. Why don't you let me have a crack at it?" She then opened her purse and pulled out an old bread bag. "Look at what else I brought."

David smiled, "bread, you brought old bread."

"What direction would you like me to throw it out at?"

"Don't throw it?" David said in a child-like voice. "You gotta stand amongst them and feed it to them evenly. That would only be fair."

Molly gets up, sits the jar on the bench along with her purse, kicks off her heels and walks passed the sidewalk onto the grass closer to the muddy edge of the pond and distributes the bread by David's direction. Ducks clambering up to her in delight. By-standers walked pass, eyeing the lady that seemed to be chatting and laughing at the air. She did not know how much time passed but it was interrupted by the sound of her phone ringing. It was Billy. She silenced it and started to walk back out to the pond, but David looked at her, almost sternly.

"I believe I have to go now." He then looks towards the direction of the light. "Do you see it? The light I mean. Do you see it."

Molly looks up. "I don't think I am meant to see it. But that is okay, because it is your time and not mine." Taking a breath, "Let's take care of this shall we."

Molly picks up the jar of ashes and walks to the pond. "Any last words?"

"Can't think of any really."

"Well, okay." Molly opened the jar and began to gently shake out the ashes into the water, many of them blowing towards the right, the direction of the wind. "Ashes to ashes, dust to dust, go in love, I shall trust."

"I like that," David said, then quietly, are you going to be, okay?"

"I am." Molly said with a smile.

David smiled back as he slowly vanished whispering, "that's right, because you are a BBBA."

52

The Pied Piper's Prince

"I see her. Her arms opened wide, and she is smiling. My beautiful boy. My sweet, beautiful boy."

"I love you mom."

53

2001

"How was the funeral?" Billy asked in a ruff voice.

"Small but nice. Real nice." Molly was trying to hide how choked up she was. "I'm glad they invited me."

"Well, it is the least they can do since it if wasn't for you he'd wouldn't be found."

"Yeah," Molly said with a painful grimace."

"You, okay? You don't sound so good."

"Fine, I guess, I started bleeding again. I wish it would stop."

"It sounds like you need to go ahead and get that hysterectomy like the doctor suggest."

Molly grimaced again while she fumbled with her door key. "First thing is first. My lease is up in three weeks, and I'm ready to move out of here."

"Into our new Galveston home!" Billy said with delightful glee.

"Yeah, but right now I think I need to lay down." Billy could hear thudding sounds as Molly entered the house, dropping her things in a trail as she made her way to the bathroom.

"How bad is it? The blood that is. How bad?"

"Well, I am going to soak in a hot tub for a bit to see if I can stop the flow for a while."

"Look, I got some things I got to finish here and then I'm gonna go home and shower and I will be right over. You rest. Do you want me to bring you anything?"

"A new uterus would be nice."

"If I can get that through the McDonald's drive through, it is yours."

Molly let out a little laugh. "Just bring yourself and your strength. I think I need you to help me pack up these boxes."

"You're already packing?"

"Like I said, I am ready to get out of here."

Molly then set her phone down on the bathroom counter, unbuttons her dress and lets it drop to the ground. She peels off her once cotton white panties and makes the decision to toss them. Turns on the bathtub water, and lets it get to a temperature she could stand while she examines herself in the mirror. Her face was starting to ashen, and she looks down to see a puddle of red on the linoleum. Geez, she takes hold of the shower rack and dips her feet in one by one before gently pulling herself down into the water, closing her eyes while ignoring the heavy breath sounds etching from the doorway.

54

Beyond the Vale

"You little prick. I can't believe you did it. Would've have never thought you had it in ya."

"Mama! I'm sorry mama! I had to. I killed Cory. Didn't have a choice mama. I killed him."

"Look at him. The little pussy."

Molly ignores Dennison, choosing to stay focused on the scene as it unfolded. "So, this is how it happened," she murmurs.

"So now you have it. All the filth for your little book."

"Those boys, who hadn't even finished high school, gone to a dance or driven a car and you had them out committing murders."

"What do you know? They wanted to do it. They got off on the power of it."

"So did you."

"What?" Molly began to laugh as a beast approaches them. "You idiot." Molly points. "Here, all this time you thought you were in control. But look who was controlling you. You are the stupid pussy. Not even capable of a single thought of your own." She stomps into his space finding that she can poke him in the chest without her hand going through him. "Well look here, you can't get away from me."

The devilish creature snarled as she laughed. "You think that you were the domesticated evil. That it was within your command to unleash your fury and your lustful temptations and that those boys were puppets on the string you mastered. You are wrong." Dennison hissed at her, but Molly kept on prodding. "There was a demonic force controlling you all along. One that you have always known was there and yet you deny it like everything was your own doing."

"You stupid girl. You are wrong."

"Wouldn't it be fitting that here you are, a woman hater despising all of woman including your own mother."

"That is not true. I did everything to please her. I quit the army so I could help her run…"

"Hah! You sound like you almost believe that hogwash. Got news for you honey, you were about to get kicked out for being a homosexual. Gay, a fag. They didn't want you around."

"Shut up! You don't know what you are saying."

"Your mommy left because she was ashamed. She already lost one husband because of your sorry ass. Yes, that's right. He called you out on your royal gayness. You made him sick."

"Shut up!"

"You made your mom sick."

"Shut the fuck up!"

"You are a sick twisted rapist and a killer."

"SHUT UPPPPPP!"

"You may have destroyed their lives, but your soul was eaten up by Satan a long time ago and even he is disgusted by what a pervert of a man you are. Oh, wait, you can't even be called a man."

Dennison lifted up his arm, he sprung down on her, it sliced right though her without making a mark.

Molly laughed.

The Beast laughed.

55

2001

"Her pulse is faint. We need to get her on the gurney and start an IV transfusion." The paramedic acted quickly with confidence. Billy sat on the bed, got up, then got back and began pacing.

"What hospital are you taking her too. Bayshore?"

"No, there trauma unit isn't incredibly good. Let's go ahead and transport her to Baytown." Looking up, "she got family you can call."

Billy rubbed his beard, "yes, I can call her mom. I just need her phone." He sees it on the bathroom counter, passed the paramedics, the gurney, the nude unconscious body of Molly. "Is she gonna make it?"

"I don't know. She has lost a lot of blood," the confident medic said sympathetically. "We will do the best we can."

The two male paramedics that had turned Molly over, covered her up with a sheet. Her eyes fluttered open momentarily. Billy saw the quick glimpse of blue green of her eyes and runs to her. "Hi," he said, taking her hand.

"Sir, we gotta take her."

Molly smiled back, she wanted to say it is my turn. My turn to be the hero.

"Let's head out! Sir, we will meet you at Baytown Memorial. Call her mother."

"Okay sir." Then in a louder voice, "Molly, I'll be right behind you."

But Molly had already closed her eyes, one last time.

56

Within the Vale

"Not so brave now are you, you fat cow."

"On the contrary limp dick, I am here now. And I am going to enjoy spending the rest of eternity, Kicking your ass!"

About the Author

Gina Lynelle Schaefer is a Texas Native who drinks a lot of coffee, chases a lot of ghosts and dreams up twisted tales of horror and spirituality combined. Using a tuxedo cat as her muse and a boisterous son as her inspiration with a patient husband as support, she has managed to conjure up many a tale.

Other books by Gina Lynelle
Tenaha
Thirteenth Hour
COMA

Follow her at Ginalynelle.com
Instagram
Facebook
Twitter